SHIFTING EARTH™

BERGER BOOKS
AN IMPRINT OF
DARK HORSE COMICS

written by
Cecil Castellucci

illustrated by
Flavia Biondi

colored by
Fabiana Mascolo

lettered by
Steve Wands

For all you wild seeds...

I.

There's a particular kind of pain
when a world is dying.

You see it in your parents' eyes.

All the things they know are missing
that you don't.

And when they talk about it,
the world they describe seems
like a dream to you.

Maybe you've seen it in mine,
though I try to look to the future
and towards hope.

I keep looking for ways to help
start a change.

So did she.

MAEVE!
THERE'S NOTHING I LOVE MORE THAN MY HANDS IN THE EARTH WITH PLANT SPECIMENS.
I KNEW I'D FIND YOU MUCKING ABOUT IN THE DIRT. FIND ANYTHING?
EVAN.
THE QUESTION IS, WILL ANYTHING I FIND HELP?
DIDN'T REALIZE YOUR NEW SELL-OUT JOB WOULD BRING YOU TO THE CLIMATE CONFERENCE.
LET'S NOT FIGHT. WE'RE DOING THE SAME WORK, MAEVE.
HARDLY.
YOU CAN'T SAVE THE WORLD ALONE.
BUT I DON'T HAVE TO DO IT WITH YOU.
FAIR ENOUGH. STILL, WE COULD CATCH THE KEYNOTE TOGETHER.
NEED A HAND?
I'VE GOT THIS, EVAN.

2042 World Climate Science Conference
I WANTED TO TALK TO YOU ABOUT A JOB.
I DON'T WORK FOR CORPORATIONS.
IT'S UP YOUR ALLEY. HEAD OF WILD SEEDS COLLECTIONS FOR RECLAMATION.
I KNOW MY RESEARCH ISN'T AS USEFUL TO THESE PEOPLE AS THOSE ROCKS YOU DRILL, RAMONA, BUT I'M TALKING ABOUT *NEW WORLDS.*
THANK YOU FOR BELIEVING IN ME.
WHAT'S UP THERE IN THE STARS IS IMPORTANT IN WAYS THAT WE DON'T UNDERSTAND YET.
I LOVE YOU, ZUZI. YOU GOT THIS.
IT'S NOT JUST BEEN ONE APOCALYPTIC CLIMATE EVENT.
IT'S A SERIES OF CUMULATIVE CATASTROPHES OVER STRETCHES OF TIME THAT HAVE GROWN INTO EXPONENTIAL CASCADING DISASTERS.
THE MYSTERIES OF THESE OTHER WORLDS ARE ESSENTIAL TO US UNDERSTANDING OUR OWN HOME.
WITH A POWERFUL ENOUGH PROPULSION, WE COULD EVEN REACH BEYOND THEM AND TO THE STARS.
YOU DON'T THINK WE'VE FAILED OUR PLANET AND WE'RE NOT JUST A FLOATING GRAVEYARD?
ONLY IF PEOPLE LIKE US GIVE UP.
DON'T LISTEN TO HER.

COME SEE WHAT I'M UP TO. WE'RE ON THE VERGE OF A BREAKTHROUGH, BUT WE COULD REALLY USE A FIELD SCIENTIST LIKE YOU.
I LOOK EVERYWHERE FOR WILD VARIETIES, AND IT'S GETTING HARDER AND HARDER TO HAVE HOPE THAT THERE'S ANYTHING LEFT TO FIND.
I DON'T KNOW HOW MUCH MORE OF THIS I CAN TAKE.
EXIT
THE GOOD NEWS IS THAT LIFE WILL GO ON.
THE BAD NEWS IS THAT HUMANS MAY NOT BE PART OF THAT LIFE.
TAKE A BREATH. IT'S NOT OVER YET. KEEP UP THE FIGHT IN YOU.
IT'S LIKE BEN ALWAYS SAID. "WE SHOULD CONTINUE TO DREAM UP NEW IDEAS TO LIVE, EVEN WHEN WE FEEL LOST."
PING
so... the end is nigh. meet me for a drink?
I CAN NEVER STAY ANGRY AT YOU FOR LONG.
IT'S MY SMILE. YOU LOVE TO SEE IT.
HEY, REMEMBER WHEN YOU, ME AND BEN SAT IN THE LAST TREE ON CAMPUS FOR A WEEK SHOUTING AT THE DEAN'S OFFICE WINDOW?
HA. IT WORKED, HE LET US PLANT SOME SAPLINGS.
I LIKE YOU MAD LIKE THAT.
BODY PROXIMITY ALERT

...IN CLOSING, WITH THE CHALLENGES THAT OUR PLANET POSES TO US, I BELIEVE IN THE FUTURE WE MIGHT EVEN FIND LAND AND ROOM FOR US ALL BEYOND THE STARS.
THANK YOU FOR CONSIDERING MY FUNDING REQUEST.
ZZZZZZ
HONORABLE MADAME PREMIERE.
DR. ZUZI REED. I'M WITH THE OBSERVATIONAL SKY INSTITUTE.
I RECENTLY DISCOVERED THE NEW NINTH PLANET IN OUR SYSTEM. I WROTE YOU ABOUT IT.
I'VE BEEN TRYING TO CONNECT. MY FUNDING HAS BEEN CUT AND I NEVER HEARD--
LOOK TO THE GROUND. THERE'S A PLANET FOR YOU TO STUDY UNDER OUR FEET.
WILL A NEW PLANET STOP THE FLOODS? THE STORMS?
NO...
SCIENCE MUST BE OF USE.
NOW IF YOU'LL EXCUSE ME, I'M SURE YOU CAN APPRECIATE THAT I WANT TO TAKE IN THIS CLEAR NIGHT WHILE IT'S HERE.
IF YOU LOOK, THERE ARE DREAMERS EVERYWHERE.

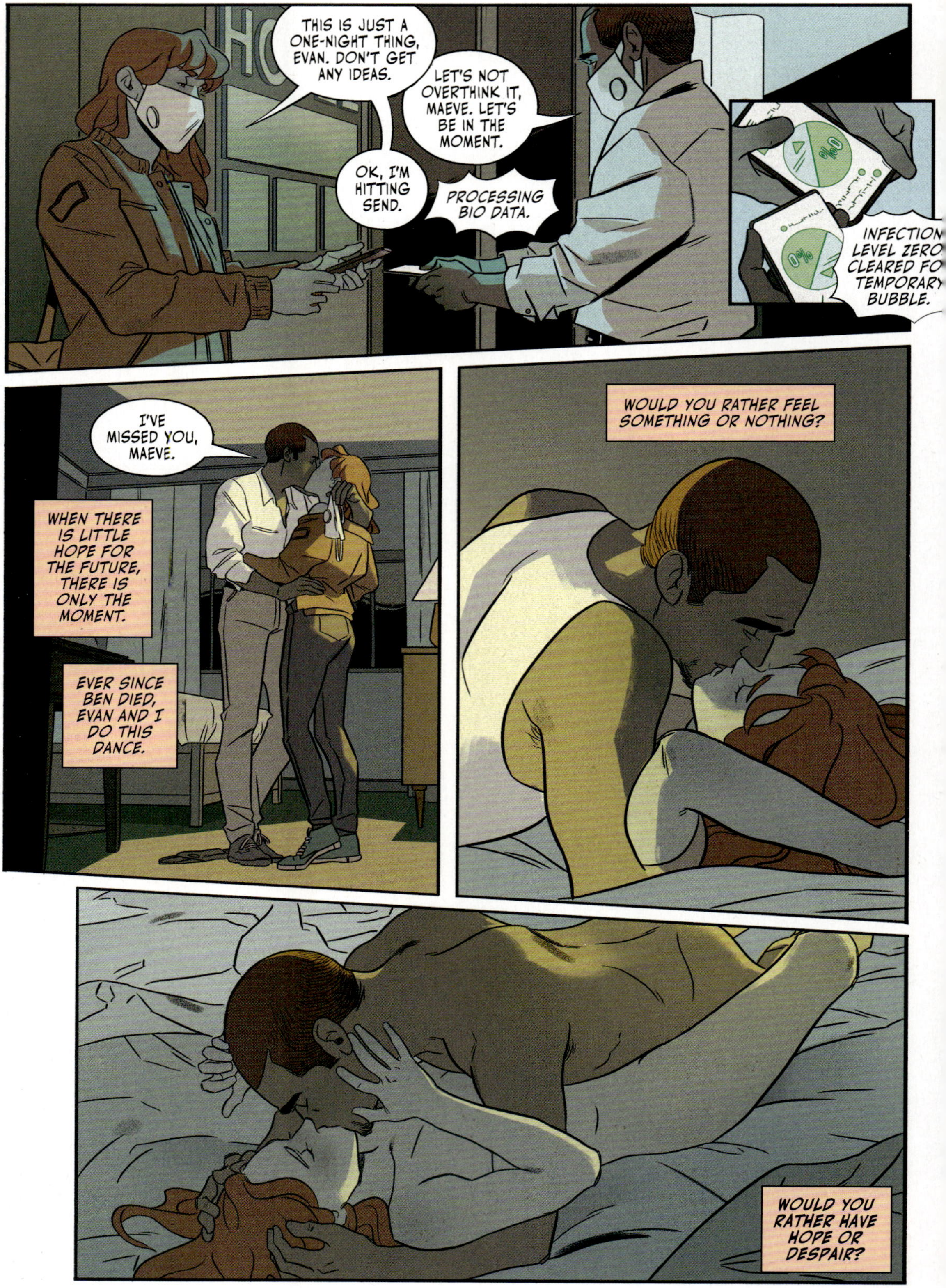
THIS IS JUST A ONE-NIGHT THING, EVAN. DON'T GET ANY IDEAS.
LET'S NOT OVERTHINK IT, MAEVE. LET'S BE IN THE MOMENT.
OK, I'M HITTING SEND.
PROCESSING BIO DATA.
INFECTION LEVEL ZERO CLEARED FO TEMPORARY BUBBLE.
I'VE MISSED YOU, MAEVE.
WHEN THERE IS LITTLE HOPE FOR THE FUTURE, THERE IS ONLY THE MOMENT.
EVER SINCE BEN DIED, EVAN AND I DO THIS DANCE.
WOULD YOU RATHER FEEL SOMETHING OR NOTHING?
WOULD YOU RATHER HAVE HOPE OR DESPAIR?

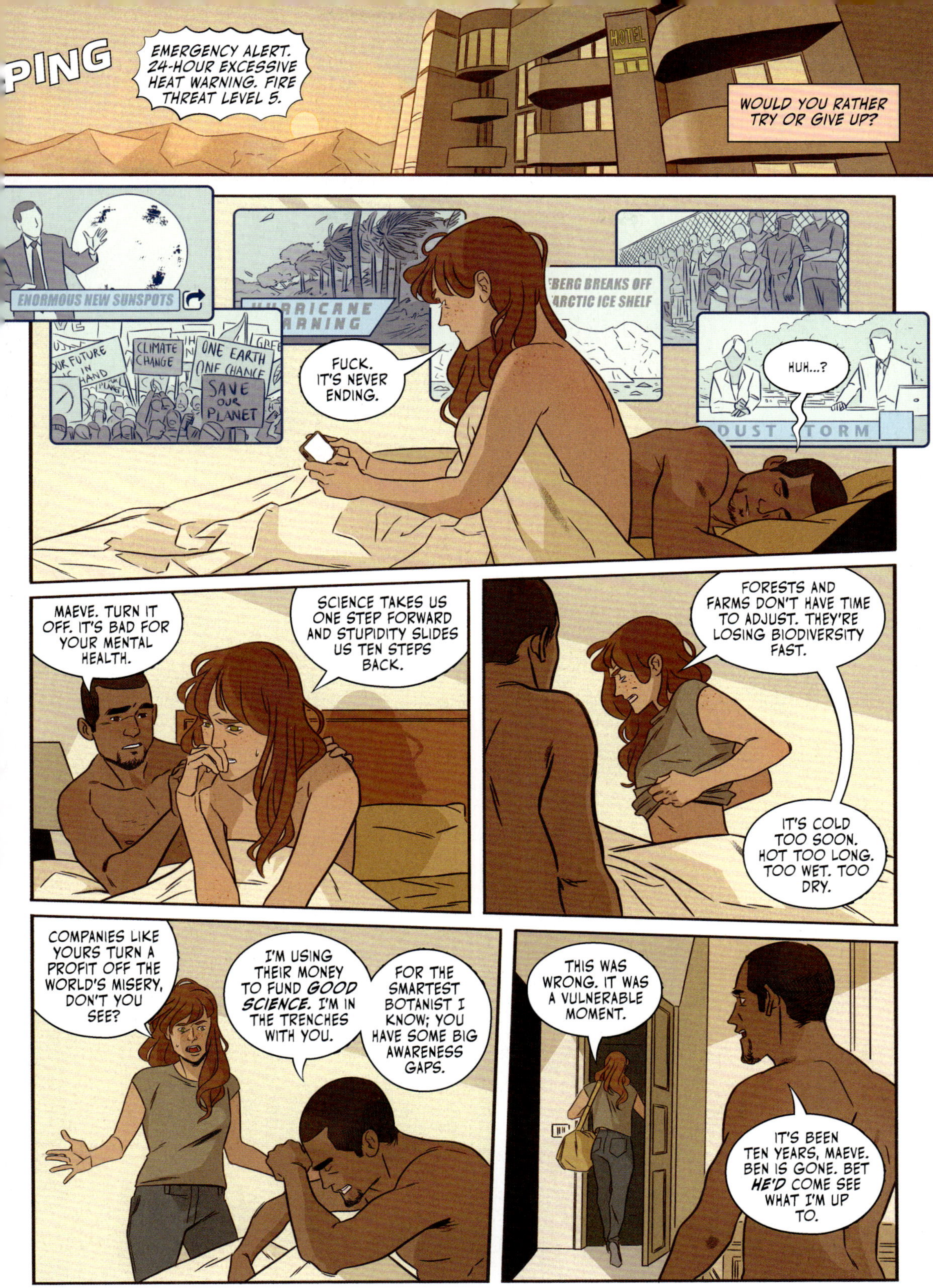
PING
EMERGENCY ALERT. 24-HOUR EXCESSIVE HEAT WARNING. FIRE THREAT LEVEL 5.
HOTEL
WOULD YOU RATHER TRY OR GIVE UP?
ENORMOUS NEW SUNSPOTS
HURRICANE WARNING
BERG BREAKS OFF ARCTIC ICE SHELF
CLIMATE CHANGE
ONE EARTH ONE CHANCE
SAVE OUR PLANET
FUCK. IT'S NEVER ENDING.
HUH...?
DUST STORM
MAEVE. TURN IT OFF. IT'S BAD FOR YOUR MENTAL HEALTH.
SCIENCE TAKES US ONE STEP FORWARD AND STUPIDITY SLIDES US TEN STEPS BACK.
FORESTS AND FARMS DON'T HAVE TIME TO ADJUST. THEY'RE LOSING BIODIVERSITY FAST.
IT'S COLD TOO SOON. HOT TOO LONG. TOO WET. TOO DRY.
COMPANIES LIKE YOURS TURN A PROFIT OFF THE WORLD'S MISERY, DON'T YOU SEE?
I'M USING THEIR MONEY TO FUND *GOOD SCIENCE*. I'M IN THE TRENCHES WITH YOU.
FOR THE SMARTEST BOTANIST I KNOW; YOU HAVE SOME BIG AWARENESS GAPS.
THIS WAS WRONG. IT WAS A VULNERABLE MOMENT.
IT'S BEEN TEN YEARS, MAEVE. BEN IS GONE. BET *HE'D* COME SEE WHAT I'M UP TO.

AS WE ALL KNOW, ONLY A DOZEN CROPS PROVIDE THREE QUARTERS OF THE WORLD'S FOOD.
WHAT'S WORSE, INDUSTRIALIZED AGRICULTURE HAS REDUCED THEIR GENETIC DIVERSITY, LEAVING THEM AND US VULNERABLE TO CLIMATE THREATS LIKE PESTS, PATHOGENS, SOIL DEGRADATION, AND CHAOTIC GROWING SEASONS.
AT GERMLINE INDUSTRIES, WE USE STATE-OF-THE ART TECHNOLOGY TO PROTECT OUR FOOD SUPPLY.
WE COLLECT, INTRODUCE, AND MODIFY GENES TO CREATE CROPS THAT WILL NOT ONLY *WITHSTAND* THESE THREATS, BUT ALSO HAVE HIGHER GERMINATION RATES, FASTER GROWTH, AND GREATER YIELDS.
GERMLINE IS SOLVING GLOBAL FOOD INSECURITY FOR TODAY AND THE FUTURE.
DANGER
KEEP OUT
CAN WE TAKE A SAMPLE FROM THAT LONE TREE?
PROP
NO TRES
THAT'S A GOVERNMENT SECURE AREA. OFF LIMITS FOR SAMPLES.
IF GERMLINE IS SERIOUS ABOUT LOOKING FOR WILD SEEDS AND OUTLIERS, NO AREA SHOULD BE OFF LIMITS.
etry
passing
YOU NEVER KNOW WHERE SOMETHING CRUCIAL MIGHT BE.
THANK YOU FOR YOUR INSIGHT, DR. LINDHOLM...

GERMLINE CONVERTED A NUCLEAR ERA BUNKER FOR ITS USE. THE SEED BANK SHARES THE BUILDING WITH THE PHYSICS DEPARTMENT.
I REALLY WANT TO GET A CLOSER LOOK AT THAT TREE.
EVERY ADVENTURE STARTS WITH A GLITCH IN THE PLAN.
SEEMS LIKE A WASTE OF LAND. SHOULD BE RECLAIMED.
EXPERIMENT FARM
THIS IS CLASSIFIED BUT THE SUPERCOLLIDER RUNS UNDER THERE. THE PHYSICISTS SAY IT COULD THROW OUR SOIL MEASUREMENTS OFF.
HUH.
THAT SOUNDS LIKE BULLSHIT.
I'D WANT ACCESS TO LOOK AT ALL SOIL, ALL PLANTS, NO MATTER WHERE THEY ARE. EVEN IF THE FEDS DON'T WANT US LOOKING.
DOES THAT MEAN YOU'RE IMPRESSED WITH WHAT I'M DOING?
LET'S NOT GET AHEAD OF OURSELVES, EVAN.
SORRY YOU CAME UP DRY. I'LL TALK TO THE ACADEMY WHEN I'M NEXT IN THE CITY. I COULD CARVE SOME FUNDS OUT FROM MY WORK.
SOME ROCK FORMATIONS ON A PLANET THAT NO ONE GIVES A SHIT ABOUT HARDLY QUALIFIES FOR FOR GEOLOGY RESEARCH.

IT'S THE BEST I CAN OFFER. IT COULD BUY YOU SOME TIME.
MY WORK *IS* OF USE. ASTROPHYSICS, SPACE, CELESTIAL MECHANICS ARE IMPORTANT.
I NEED TO GET TO THE OBSERVATORY BEFORE THE SKIES TURN.
IF YOU HAVE TO GO, TAKE THE MOTOR.
WILL IT BE FAST ENOUGH TO BEAT THE STORM?
I'VE MADE SOME MODIFICATIONS. BEEN EXPERIMENTING WITH NEW COMBUSTIONS.
OF COURSE, YOU HAVE.
YOU'LL SEE IT'S GOT SOME KICK TO IT.
BUT, IF THE WIND STARTS TO GALE, PULL OVER AND TURN IT OFF. I'M WORRIED ABOUT SPARKS.
ARE YOU USING ANY IN SITU CONSERVATION PRACTICES? SEED TRANSFER ZONES?
ONE DISEASE COULD WIPE OUT AN ENTIRE SPECIES BECAUSE THEY'RE TOO MUCH ALIKE.
WE'RE FOCUSING ON MANIPULATING THE DNA OF HIGH YIELD FOODSTUFFS TO GROW UNDER ANY CONDITIONS.
YOU'D BE SCOUTING FOR WILD RELATIVES OF STAPLE CROPS. HERE'S OUR COLLECTION SO FAR.
THIS IS IT? I'VE GOT MORE VARIETIES IN MY HOTEL ROOM.

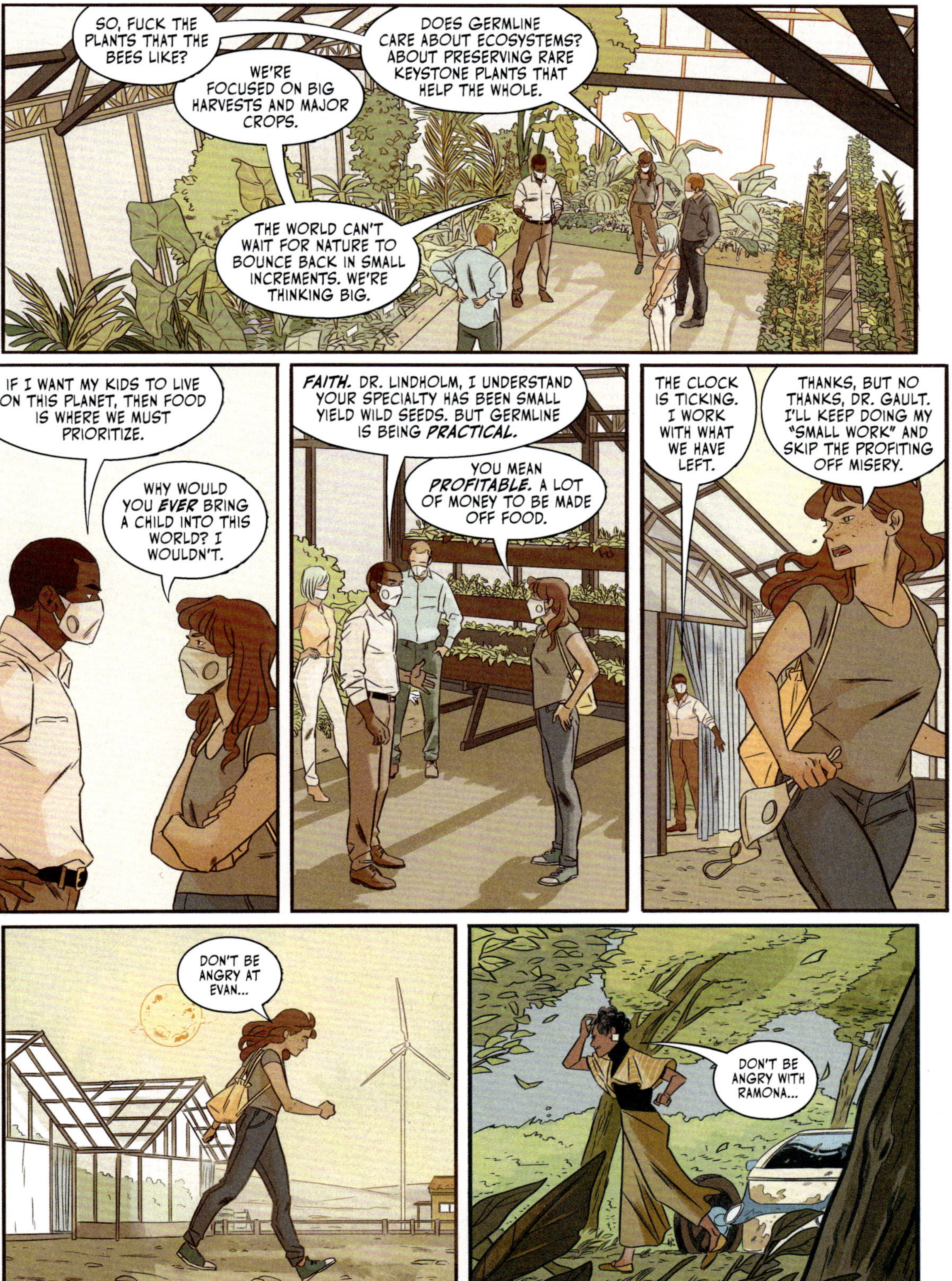
SO, FUCK THE PLANTS THAT THE BEES LIKE?
WE'RE FOCUSED ON BIG HARVESTS AND MAJOR CROPS.
DOES GERMLINE CARE ABOUT ECOSYSTEMS? ABOUT PRESERVING RARE KEYSTONE PLANTS THAT HELP THE WHOLE.
THE WORLD CAN'T WAIT FOR NATURE TO BOUNCE BACK IN SMALL INCREMENTS. WE'RE THINKING BIG.
IF I WANT MY KIDS TO LIVE ON THIS PLANET, THEN FOOD IS WHERE WE MUST PRIORITIZE.
WHY WOULD YOU EVER BRING A CHILD INTO THIS WORLD? I WOULDN'T.
FAITH. DR. LINDHOLM, I UNDERSTAND YOUR SPECIALTY HAS BEEN SMALL YIELD WILD SEEDS. BUT GERMLINE IS BEING PRACTICAL.
YOU MEAN PROFITABLE. A LOT OF MONEY TO BE MADE OFF FOOD.
THE CLOCK IS TICKING. I WORK WITH WHAT WE HAVE LEFT.
THANKS, BUT NO THANKS, DR. GAULT. I'LL KEEP DOING MY "SMALL WORK" AND SKIP THE PROFITING OFF MISERY.
DON'T BE ANGRY AT EVAN...
DON'T BE ANGRY WITH RAMONA...

LOOK WHERE THEY WON'T LET YOU AND YOU MIGHT FIND SOMETHING INTERESTING.
NO TRESPASSING
THIS TREE DOESN'T HAVE THE RIGHT CONDITIONS TO BE THRIVING HERE.
WHERE DID YOU COME FROM?
WHEN WE TRESPASS INTO THE UNKNOWN, THINGS MOVE FORWARD.
CLIK
ENDANGERED
EVEN IF THE PATH AHEAD IS CLOUDED WITH MYSTERY.
OMIGOD, THE SUN.
BY THE SIBLINGS!

WOOOOO WOOOOO
WHAT'S GOING ON? WHAT HAPPENED TO THE POWER?
WE SHUT DOWN NON-ESSENTIALS DUE TO A CORONAL MASS EJECTION. WE NEED TO CLEAR THE AREA FROM THE COLLIDER TILL THE PARTICLES PASS.
ONE OF MY COLLEAGUES TOOK A WALK. SHE CAN'T BE FAR. I'LL BE QUICK!
HURRY! PROTECT THE EQUIPMENT PROTO-TYPES. I DON'T WANT TO LOSE OUR WORK.
WE SHOULD GO INTO A SHELTER, SIR. LOOKS LIKE A CATEGORY 7!
I CAN'T BELIEVE WHAT I'M SEEING. THIS SPECIES SPECIALIZES ON SOUTH-FACING ROCKY SLOPES, BUT THIS IS BOTTOMLAND.
ENDANGERED
5% CERTAINTY: OUT OF ZONE
ENDANGERED
THIS ISN'T SUPPOSED TO GROW HERE.

BRACE FOR WAVE ONE IMPACT.
I'VE NEVER SEEN PARTICLES LIKE THAT.
THE CORONAL MASS EJECTION FROM THE SUN MUST BE CHANGING THEIR FLAVOR.
SHUT IT DOWN! WE CAN'T HAVE THAT EXOTIC PARTICLE VARIABLE IN THE COLLIDER!

MY SKIN...
...IT'S BUBBLING...
THE SUN SHOULD NEVER BE TAKEN FOR GRANTED.
FOR IT DOES NOT SIT QUIETLY IN THE SKY.

MAEVE! MAEVE! GET OUT OF THERE!
DR. GAULT, WE MUST GET INSIDE IN CASE THERE IS A COLLIDER BREACH!
OBSERVATION 7th moon, Third Day, Cycle 55, 17:23 Looks like a tear in the sky Constellations—incorrect position one year off?
THAT MAKES NO SENSE.
DID OUR DIGGING MACHINE DO THAT TO THE SKY?
UNLIKELY. I'LL GO CHECK IT OUT. PROBABLY A FLURRY OF MICRO STORMS.
QUICK, GET SOME SHELTER!
GET IT OFF ME! AAAHH!
EVAN! HELP, I'M STUCK!

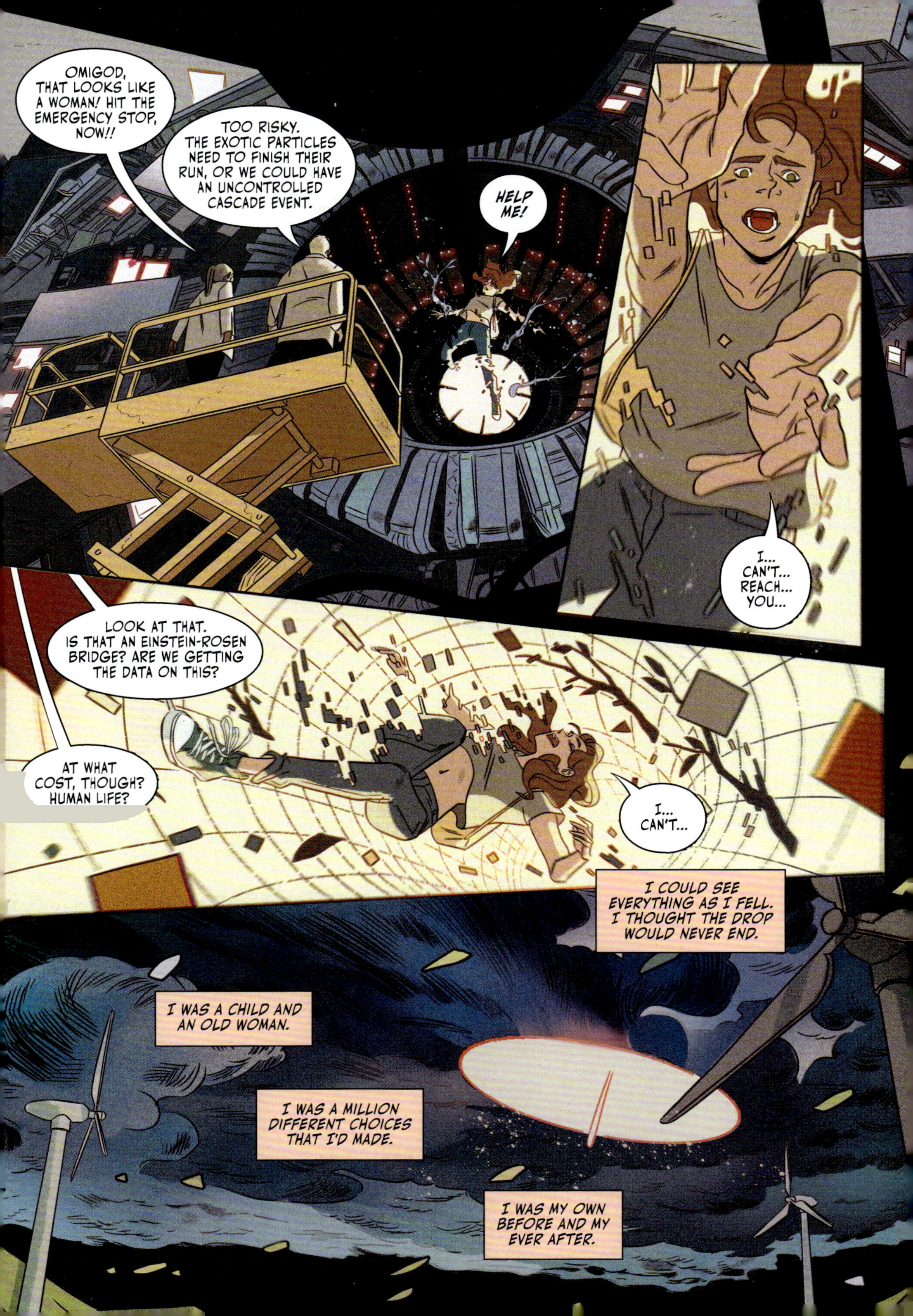
OMIGOD, THAT LOOKS LIKE A WOMAN! HIT THE EMERGENCY STOP, NOW!!
TOO RISKY. THE EXOTIC PARTICLES NEED TO FINISH THEIR RUN, OR WE COULD HAVE AN UNCONTROLLED CASCADE EVENT.
HELP ME!
I... CAN'T... REACH... YOU...
LOOK AT THAT. IS THAT AN EINSTEIN-ROSEN BRIDGE? ARE WE GETTING THE DATA ON THIS?
AT WHAT COST, THOUGH? HUMAN LIFE?
I... CAN'T...
I COULD SEE EVERYTHING AS I FELL. I THOUGHT THE DROP WOULD NEVER END.
I WAS A CHILD AND AN OLD WOMAN.
I WAS A MILLION DIFFERENT CHOICES THAT I'D MADE.
I WAS MY OWN BEFORE AND MY EVER AFTER.

OBSERVATION 7th moon, Third Day, Cycle 55, 18:18 Unknown object - not a meteor
MY MIND AND EYES!
CALCULATE LANDING. GET THERE FIRST. THIS IS MY FIND.
IN THAT MOMENT, THOUGH I DID NOT KNOW IT YET, I WAS REBORN.

HELP!
BEN? IS THAT YOU? DO YOU SEE THIS? IS THIS REAL?
I CAN'T TOUCH THE GROUND...ON MY OWN.
AM I SICK? IS THIS THE FEVER?
YOU'RE THROUGH. YOU'RE OK.
IT'S SO GREEN. EVERYTHING IS SO ALIVE. INCLUDING YOU.
I MUST BE DREAMING.

BEEEP BEEEEP BEEEEP BEEEP
COME ON YOU SOUPED UP THING. GO FASTER.
DON'T LOSE THE SIGNAL. DON'T LOSE IT!
DR. GAULT, I THOUGHT THIS WAS AN EMPTY FIELD. WHERE DID THESE TREES COME FROM?
THOSE ARE DRY, BUT THIS TREE IS THRIVING...
BY THE MOONS, IT'S LIKE A HOLE IN THE WORLD.
LOOK AT THE ROOTS, THEY'RE GLOWING.
OH MY MONSTROUS.
A FLYING BEAST!
SWEPT FROM AN UNKNOWN ISLAND?
WAIT.
IT'S A FLYING *MACHINE*.

MYCELIUM TRACES. FUNGI NETWORK. GOOD BARK. WET SEASONS. THEIR ROOT COMMUNICATION MUST BE VERY STRONG. LOOK AT THE SAPLINGS.
I REMEMBER TRYING TO SAVE THIS SPECIES WHEN WE WERE IN COLLEGE, BEN. BEFORE YOU GOT SICK.
DON'T MOVE.
IS THAT A GUN? IT LOOKS LIKE A TOY.
BEN...
WHO ARE YOU? WHERE DID YOU COME FROM?
WHAT KIND OF TECH WAS THAT?
HOW DO YOU KNOW MY NAME?
ARE YOU SPYING ON US? WHAT IS THAT DOOR YOU CAME THROUGH?
LOOK. NO SIGN OF BARK BEETLE OUTBREAK.
WHY ARE YOU IN THIS ZONE?
I DON'T FEEL RIGHT, BEN. I FEEL *OFF.*
STEP AWAY FROM THOSE LIGHT SHARDS. I FORBID YOU TO USE THEM.
I FEEL LIKE I'M ON FIRE. EVERY MOLECULE STINGS...
SWOOSH

SORRY LADY, WHOEVER YOU ARE, BUT I CAN'T TAKE ANY CHANCES.
NO LOOSE ENDS. JUST ANOTHER SAD VICTIM OF THE STORMS. GO WITH THE LAND.

IT'S SHRINKING.
I'VE WORKED TOO HARD TO GET HERE. I WON'T FEEL GUILTY FOR DOING MY DUTY.
THE MYSTERIES OF THE UNIVERSE WILL NEVER CEASE TO AMAZE ME.
EVERYTHING FEELS CONNECTED.
CAPTAIN NAGATA! WE FEARED THE WORST!
I'M ALRIGHT. THE WILDS RECLAMATION SITE ISN'T.
GONE.
ARGH.
WAIT, WHAT'S THAT?
THEY'RE *DIGGING.*

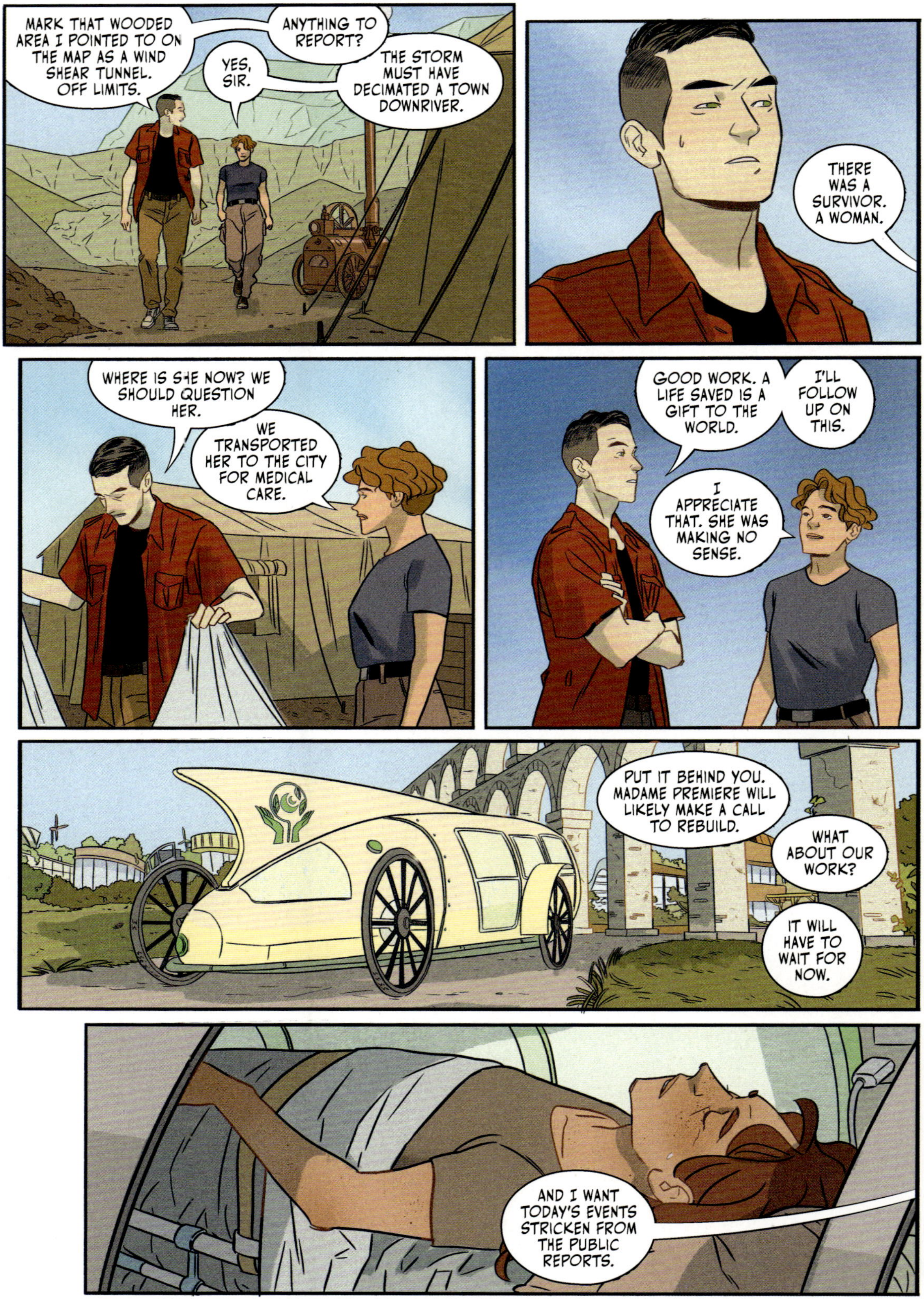
MARK THAT WOODED AREA I POINTED TO ON THE MAP AS A WIND SHEAR TUNNEL. OFF LIMITS.
YES, SIR.
ANYTHING TO REPORT?
THE STORM MUST HAVE DECIMATED A TOWN DOWNRIVER.
THERE WAS A SURVIVOR. A WOMAN.
WHERE IS SHE NOW? WE SHOULD QUESTION HER.
WE TRANSPORTED HER TO THE CITY FOR MEDICAL CARE.
GOOD WORK. A LIFE SAVED IS A GIFT TO THE WORLD.
I'LL FOLLOW UP ON THIS.
I APPRECIATE THAT. SHE WAS MAKING NO SENSE.
PUT IT BEHIND YOU. MADAME PREMIERE WILL LIKELY MAKE A CALL TO REBUILD.
WHAT ABOUT OUR WORK?
IT WILL HAVE TO WAIT FOR NOW.
AND I WANT TODAY'S EVENTS STRICKEN FROM THE PUBLIC REPORTS.

2.

My parents were the kind of people
who bought the last of things
so that I would have the memory
of them.

They thought they were doing me
a kindness by shielding me from
how hard it had become and how
much was gone.

Instead, those last tastes I had of
things only made me feel the pain
of their loss even more.

The world was not well.

It had been stripped bare and
I would not let it happen again.

You need to know that.

MAGNETIC SHIFTS. MICRO SHEARS. WE HAVE WEATHERED MANY STORMS. YET SOMETHING IS DIFFERENT THIS CYCLE.
MORE SMALL ISLANDS AND ATOLLS THAN USUAL HAVE BEEN LOST.
A BRUTAL CYCLE 55 IS UPON US.
"OUR BEST PEOPLE HAVE BEEN DEPLOYED TO HELP REBUILD.
"WE CANNOT AFFORD TO LOSE MORE LAND TO THE RAGING WATERS OR WINDS.
"AS A LARGER ISLAND, LAURENTIA, WILL DO WHAT WE CAN TO HELP THE DISPLACED, AND HONOR OUR EXCHANGES.
"BUT WE MUST TEND TO OUR OWN PEOPLE FIRST.
"AND MAKE USE OF EVERY UNTAPPED ADVANTAGE OUR RESOURCES GIFT US."
TOO LONG THE STORMS HAVE RULED US. I WANT US TO RULE THE STORMS. LAURENTIA HAS AN OBLIGATION TO LEAD OUR WORLD INTO THE FUTURE.
WE WILL RIDE OUT THIS CYCLE AND SURVIVE.

"NOTHING AND NO ONE WILL STOP OUR PROGRESS."
WHERE'S MY SPECIMEN BAG... NEED TO DO A SCRAPING OF THAT TREE...
SHE DOESN'T HAVE A VARIOLATION MARK. MUST BE BRINGER POX.
SURPRISED SHE DIDN'T HAVE IT AS A CHILD.
LUCKY, SHE LANDED HERE. OUR SHORES ARE MORE STABLE THAN MOST.
DEB HOLT? DID YOU CHANGE YOUR HAIR? HAVE I BEEN IN AN ACCIDENT?
WHERE'S MY BAG? *WHERE'S YOUR MASK?*
KEEP YOUR DISTANCE. STOP TOUCHING ME!
PLEASE CALM DOWN. WE'RE TRYING TO HELP YOU.
SHE'S BABBLING. STAGE THREE OF BRINGER. DELIRIUM.
CHANCES?
BRINGER IS MUCH MORE DANGEROUS AS AN ADULT.
I'LL PREP THE PAPERWORK FOR BODY TRANSFER AND RECYCLING JUST IN CASE.
DID YOU SEE HER ROUGH HANDS? I WONDER WHAT HER *USE* WAS?

"I'VE READ THE REPORTS ABOUT THIS CYCLE.
"TIDES ARE ERRATIC, KNOWN OCEAN CURRENTS ARE COLLAPSING, TRUE NORTH WOBBLES."
LAB CLOSED. REASSIGNMENT PENDING. DO NOT ENTER.
WE WON'T SURVIVE UNLESS WE CORE HEADS-- SCIENCE, ENGINEERING, LAND, EXCHANGE--COME TOGETHER WITH FRESH IDEAS.
GROW OUR SHORES. LAND IS OF USE.
WE CAN'T PROGRESS AS A SOCIETY IF WE KEEP HAVING TO REBUILD.
WE NEED TO FIND RESOURCES THAT MAKE OUR POWER INDEPENDENT OF THE ELEMENTS...
...AND OTHER ISLANDS.
NURSE? WHERE'S CALL BUTTON? I FEEL--

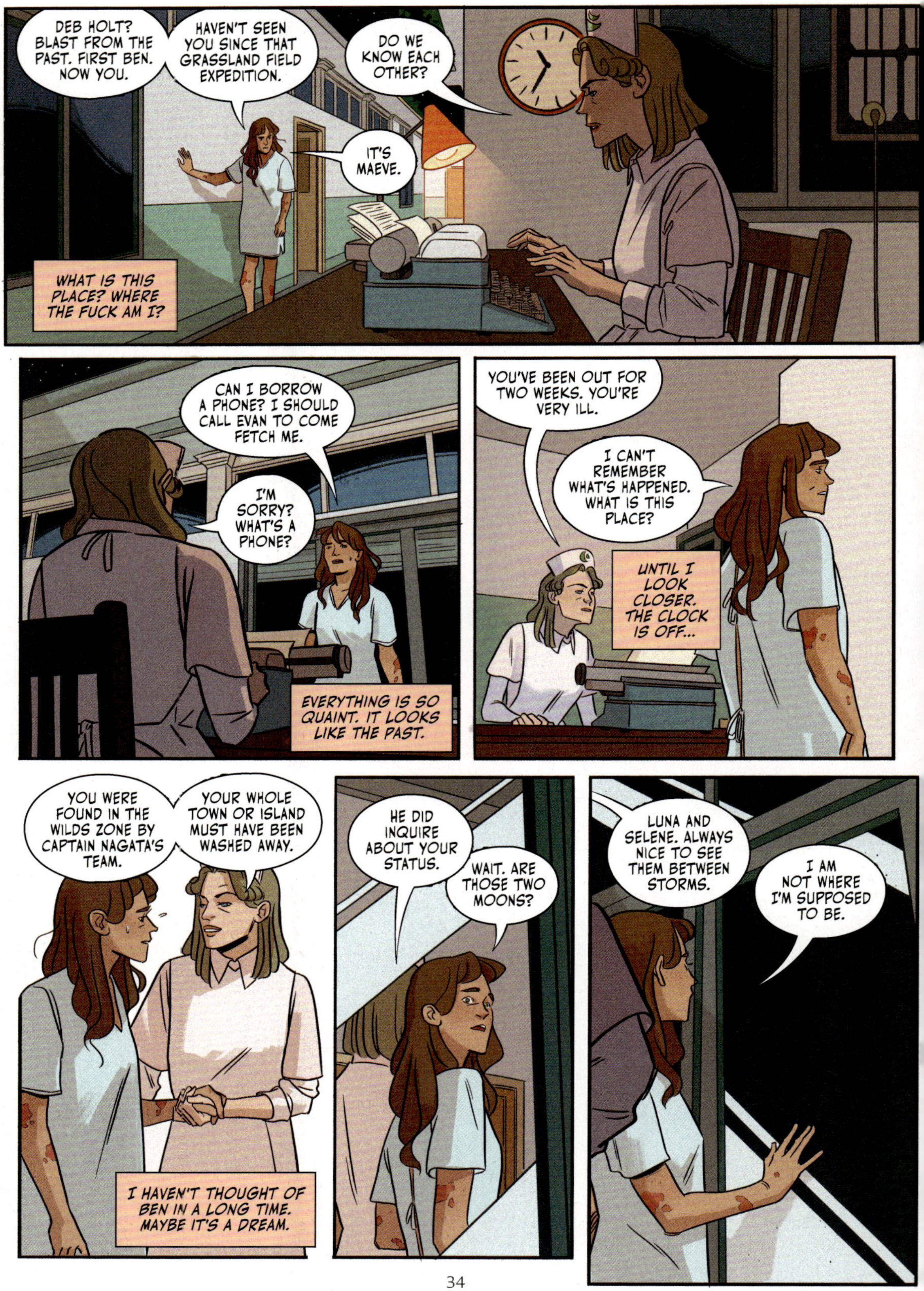
DEB HOLT? BLAST FROM THE PAST. FIRST BEN. NOW YOU.
HAVEN'T SEEN YOU SINCE THAT GRASSLAND FIELD EXPEDITION.
DO WE KNOW EACH OTHER?
IT'S MAEVE.
WHAT IS THIS PLACE? WHERE THE FUCK AM I?
CAN I BORROW A PHONE? I SHOULD CALL EVAN TO COME FETCH ME.
I'M SORRY? WHAT'S A PHONE?
EVERYTHING IS SO QUAINT. IT LOOKS LIKE THE PAST.
YOU'VE BEEN OUT FOR TWO WEEKS. YOU'RE VERY ILL.
I CAN'T REMEMBER WHAT'S HAPPENED. WHAT IS THIS PLACE?
UNTIL I LOOK CLOSER. THE CLOCK IS OFF...
YOU WERE FOUND IN THE WILDS ZONE BY CAPTAIN NAGATA'S TEAM.
YOUR WHOLE TOWN OR ISLAND MUST HAVE BEEN WASHED AWAY.
I HAVEN'T THOUGHT OF BEN IN A LONG TIME. MAYBE IT'S A DREAM.
HE DID INQUIRE ABOUT YOUR STATUS.
WAIT. ARE THOSE TWO MOONS?
LUNA AND SELENE. ALWAYS NICE TO SEE THEM BETWEEN STORMS.
I AM NOT WHERE I'M SUPPOSED TO BE.

SOMEONE, GO AFTER HER!
STEAM-POWERED WALKWAY. SOLAR PANELS. RAINWATER RECYCLING. GREEN ARCHITECTURE. IT'S A WORKING SUSTAINABLE CITY. THE KIND THAT BEN FOUGHT TO PLAN.
THIS IS THE GREEN DREAM REALIZED.
MAKE SURE TO REMEMBER EVERYTHING WHEN YOU WAKE UP.
HEY!
THE AIR IS SO CRISP. NO SMOG. A LOT OF BICYCLES. ROOFTOP BEEHIVES. MY GOD. THE STARS!
COME ON BACK WITH ME, MISS.
OW! YOU'RE HURTING ME.
THIS DOESN'T FEEL LIKE A DREAM. I SMELL. I READ. I FEEL.
WHERE AM I?
LAURENTIA. IN VERDELINA.
I'VE NEVER HEARD OF IT.
YOU'VE NEVER HEARD OF THE BIGGEST ISLAND ON THIS PART OF THE OCEAN?

OBSERVATION 7th moon, Tenth Day, Cycle 55, 21:23 Phenomena unknown. Extraplanetary? No effect from impact. Threat assessment: low? Explanation...?
THINK, ZUZI, THINK. WHAT DID YOU SEE?
OBSERVATION 7th moon, Tenth Day, Cycle 55, 26:14
Explore possible fluctuations: Energy, mass, physics, relativity, time, atoms...
SIBLING MOONS. COULD IT BE?
DID YOU SEE THE IMPOSSIBLE?

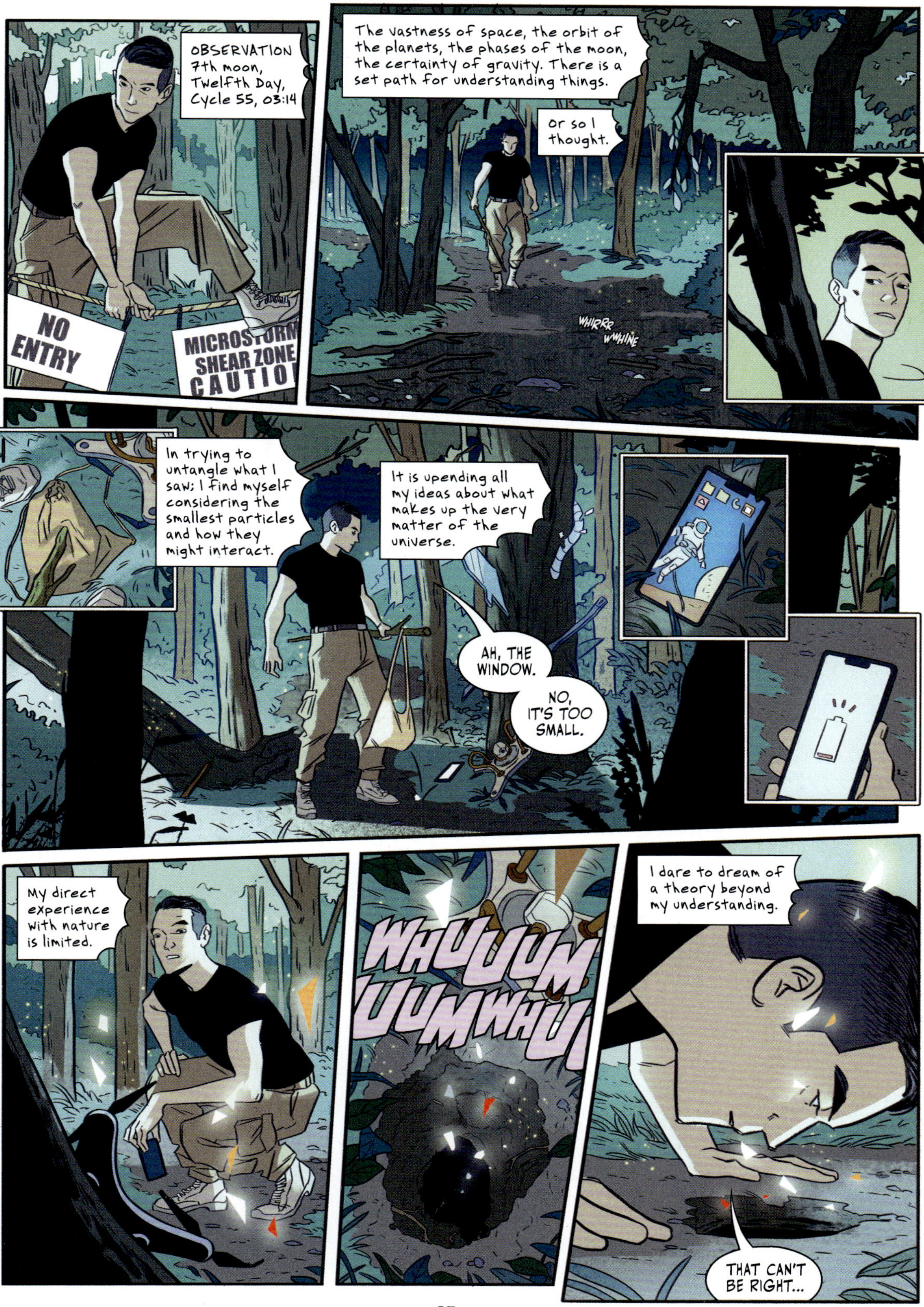
OBSERVATION
7th moon, Twelfth Day, Cycle 55, 03:14
NO ENTRY
MICROSTORM SHEAR ZONE CAUTIO
The vastness of space, the orbit of the planets, the phases of the moon, the certainty of gravity. There is a set path for understanding things.
Or so I thought.
WHIRRR
WWHINE
In trying to untangle what I saw; I find myself considering the smallest particles and how they might interact.
It is upending all my ideas about what makes up the very matter of the universe.
AH, THE WINDOW.
NO, IT'S TOO SMALL.
My direct experience with nature is limited.
WHUUUM
UUMWHU
I dare to dream of a theory beyond my understanding.
THAT CAN'T BE RIGHT...

THAT'S... IMPOSSIBLE.

Multiple worlds. Parallel worlds.
If I could get anyone to believe me.

ZUZI. HAVE YOU BEEN HOLED UP HERE SINCE I LEFT?
RRWOOF!
BANAS. GOOD BOY.
DID YOU PLEAD MY CASE FOR STAYING HERE? I HOPE MADAME PREMIERE LISTENED.
THEY WANT TO EXCHANGE YOU TO A SMALLER ISLAND.
NO. I'M NOT DOING THAT. I'M ON THE BRINK OF SOMETHING BIG.
I CONVINCED THEM THAT YOU'D DO A STINT AT A WAVES FACILITY INSTEAD.
THE WAVES. THAT'S EXILE.
I'M SORRY MY LOVE. I USED ALL THE CLOUT I HAD AND ONLY MANAGED THAT.
WHAT'S THAT ON THE BOARD?
I'M ON TO SOMETHING, RAMONA. I DON'T HAVE IT CRACKED JUST YET.
BUT IT'S REWRITING THE WORLD.
I FEEL AS THOUGH I'M SEEING REALITY FOR THE FIRST TIME.

POSSIBILITIES.
YOU'RE DREAMING.
YOU'VE HIT YOUR HEAD.
YOU'RE IN A COMA.
YOU'VE TIME TRAVELED.
THE PARTICLE COLLIDER. IT'S A PARALLEL WORLD!
FOR THE EXIT SURVEY, I NEED TO KNOW WHEN YOUR COURSES ARE. MONTHLY OR YEARLY?
YOU HAVEN'T BLED SINCE YOU'VE ARRIVED, AND IT'S BEEN FOUR MINI MOONS.
MONTHLY. LIKE CLOCKWORK. YOU'RE LETTING ME GO?
HMM. I'LL ORDER ONE OF THOSE NEW RAT TESTS. THAT'LL BE QUICKER THAN WAITING TO SEE.
I CAN'T BE PREGNANT.
WHAT A RARE BLESSING IF YOU ARE WITH CHILD.
I'M ALWAYS CAREFUL.
YOU'RE A STRANGE ONE.
I WISH MY COURSES WEREN'T YEARLY SO I'D HAVE A CHANCE.

I ALWAYS SWORE I'D NEVER BRING A CHILD INTO THIS WORLD.
I COULD REPORT YOU. BE HAPPY YOU FOUND A *USE,* OR IT WAS THE GREAT RETURN FOR YOU.
THEN AGAIN. I GUESS THIS *ISN'T* MY WORLD.
A BABY. WHAT WOULD EVAN THINK?
THIS IS NO KNOWN ISLAND TECHNOLOGY.
Dear Ramona. This can't be how my story goes. I'll perish out here.
It's so remote. I never knew the world could be so lonely.

WELCOME TO THE WAVES FACILITY, DR. REED. I'M CLAIRE.
AT LAST, I THOUGHT WE'D NEVER ARRIVE. I HAVEN'T SEEN ANOTHER ISLAND OR AN ATOLL FOR DAYS.
There is no one I can talk to. That I can call a friend.
YOU KNOW THE DEAL-- WE GENERATE POWER FOR BOATS CARRYING PEOPLE AND GOODS ON LONG HAULS FROM ISLAND TO ISLAND.
SO WOBBLY. IT'S WORSE THAN THE BOAT.
YES. WE USE THE FORCE OF THE WAVES.
A FEW MONTHS HERE, AND YOU BANK A LOT OF USEFULNESS CREDIT IN YOUR STASH.
BETTER THAN HAVING A BABY.
I PLAN ON RETURNING TO LAURENTIA *QUICKLY.*
OH, SCIENTISTS STAY INDEFINITELY. WE HAD TWO BUT ONE DIED. YOU'RE THE REPLACEMENT.
NOT MUCH OF A LAB.
YOU JUST MONITOR THE TIDAL PULLS FROM THE MOONS. I ADJUST THE RIG.
BASIC. WHO'S THAT?
THAT'S YOUR BOSS, DR. PARNAK.
I long to get home. Before my brain degenerates.
"DON'T WAKE HIM. HE'LL BITE YOUR HEAD OFF."
I'M IN HELL.
BUT AT LEAST I CAN SEE THE STARS.

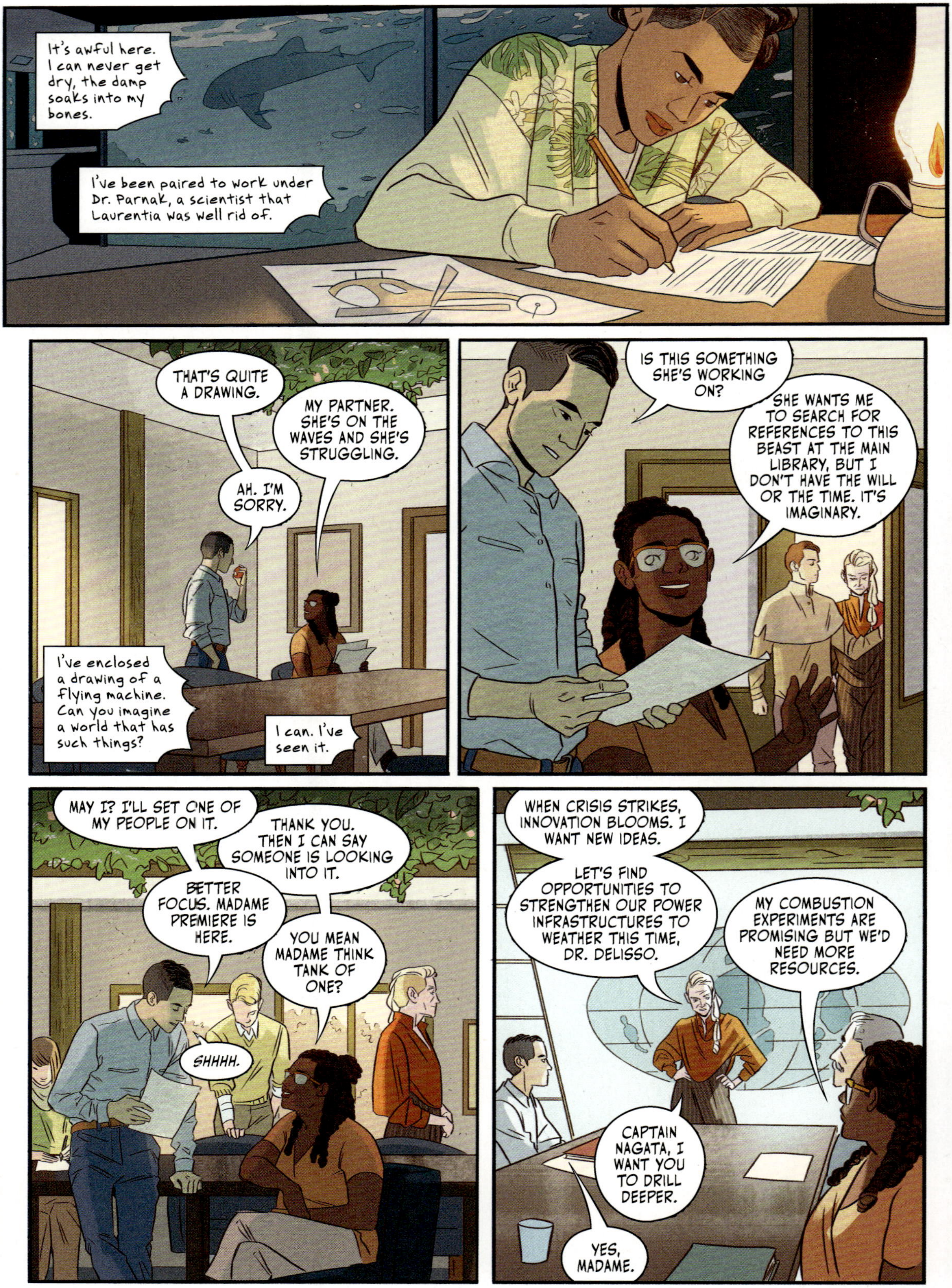
It's awful here. I can never get dry, the damp soaks into my bones.
I've been paired to work under Dr. Parnak, a scientist that Laurentia was well rid of.
THAT'S QUITE A DRAWING.
MY PARTNER. SHE'S ON THE WAVES AND SHE'S STRUGGLING.
AH. I'M SORRY.
I've enclosed a drawing of a flying machine. Can you imagine a world that has such things?
I can. I've seen it.
IS THIS SOMETHING SHE'S WORKING ON?
SHE WANTS ME TO SEARCH FOR REFERENCES TO THIS BEAST AT THE MAIN LIBRARY, BUT I DON'T HAVE THE WILL OR THE TIME. IT'S IMAGINARY.
MAY I? I'LL SET ONE OF MY PEOPLE ON IT.
THANK YOU. THEN I CAN SAY SOMEONE IS LOOKING INTO IT.
BETTER FOCUS. MADAME PREMIERE IS HERE.
YOU MEAN MADAME THINK TANK OF ONE?
SHHHH.
WHEN CRISIS STRIKES, INNOVATION BLOOMS. I WANT NEW IDEAS.
LET'S FIND OPPORTUNITIES TO STRENGTHEN OUR POWER INFRASTRUCTURES TO WEATHER THIS TIME, DR. DELISSO.
MY COMBUSTION EXPERIMENTS ARE PROMISING BUT WE'D NEED MORE RESOURCES.
CAPTAIN NAGATA, I WANT YOU TO DRILL DEEPER.
YES, MADAME.

"THIS IS NOT THE TIME TO BE CAUTIOUS, CAPTAIN NAGATA. WE MUST ACT QUICKLY TO FIND NEW WAYS FORWARD IN UNCERTAIN TIMES.
"WE HAVE A MORAL OBLIGATION TO ENSURE OUR OWN ISLAND'S SURVIVAL."
ERGOVERNMENT AL PANEL ON LIMATE CHANGE
INCREASE EXTREME EVENTS I WARMIN
GLOBAL WARMIN
HUH.
KNOCK KNOCK
CAPTAIN NAGATA. I TRACKED DOWN THE UNIDENTIFIED WOMAN WE FOUND AT THE SITE.
YOU WERE RIGHT. THEY *HAD* MOVED HER.
THANK YOU. I'LL FOLLOW UP.
SHE CAN TELL ME EXACTLY WHAT I'M LOOKING AT HERE.
ENTS IN A WARMING WORLD
ADVANCEMENT OR INVASION.

TOOK YOU LONG ENOUGH TO FOLLOW UP. BUT I SUPPOSE A PERSON AT YOUR LEVEL IS BUSY.
WHY IS SHE BEING KEPT IN THIS WING?
WE HAD TO LOCK HER IN WITH THE UNWILLING MOTHERS WHO RUN. SHE KEPT TRYING TO FIND A WAY HOME.
BUT CAN'T SAY WHERE IT IS OR HOW TO GET THERE. DOESN'T KNOW ANYTHING ABOUT HERSELF.
THERE'S TO BE NO MORE TRANSFERS WITHOUT MY AUTHORITY.
OH, I SEE. YOU'RE THE FATHER. YOU HERE TO BOND?
THAT'S WHY SHE SAYS SHE KNOWS YOU. SAYS SHE KNOWS ME, TOO.
APOLOGIES THAT IT TOOK ME A WHILE TO COME SEE YOU.
BEN. IT'S *REALLY* YOU. I THOUGHT IT WAS A DREAM.
I THINK WE GOT OFF ON THE WRONG FOOT.
YOU THINK? YOU ALWAYS HAD THIS UNCANNY WAY OF SURPRISING ME.
LET'S GO HAVE A TALK.

I FIND IT DISTURBING THAT YOU THINK YOU KNOW ME WHEN WE'VE NEVER MET.
HAVEN'T WE?
DO YOU REMEMBER YOUR NAME? PERHAPS THAT WILL RING A BELL.
MAEVE LINDHOLM.
I'D STARTED TO FORGET YOU. THAT'S WHAT DEATH DOES. PEOPLE FADE FROM MEMORY.
IT'S HARD TO LOOK AT YOU.
I'D LIKE TO MAKE SENSE OF THIS.
HOW ABOUT YOU START WITH HOW I DIED IN THIS SO-CALLED WORLD OF YOURS.
arth. Ten
ears ago.
DID YOU HEAR ABOUT THE DUST STORM OUT WEST? CROPS RUINED.
IF THERE WAS A WAY TO GET THEM TO BEND MORE, THEY WOULDN'T BREAK IN THOSE WINDS.
OR REDUCE DESICCATION.
YOUR VOICE IS FROGGY.
THE MORE WARMING THAT HAPPENS, THE MORE NEW DISEASES ARE GOING TO COME. NO ONE IS SAFE.
WASHING HANDS
STAYNG APART
WE'RE ALMOST AT THE HOSPITAL. JUST A BIT FURTHER.
I DIDN'T GET TO SAY GOODBYE, EVAN.
I WISH I COULD BE THERE IN PERSON WITH YOU. YOU'RE GOING TO SURVIVE THIS.
I WON'T. HOW CAN I LIVE IN A WORLD THAT DOESN'T INCLUDE BEN?

THERE ARE THINGS I SAW WHEN I PULLED YOU THROUGH. TECHNOLOGY I'VE NEVER SEEN BEFORE. SHARDS OF LIGHT. STARS...
I DON'T KNOW THAT I SHOULD BE TALKING TO YOU. I DON'T KNOW HOW THINGS WORK HERE.
IT'S BEN AND NOT BEN.
I'M THE ONLY ADVOCATE YOU HAVE HERE.
THOSE MACHINES I PULLED YOU FROM. WHAT WERE THEY?
I CAN SEE THE ECHOES OF HIM.
THE BOOK IN YOUR BAG. THE PICTURES IN IT. ARE THEY REAL? WHAT IS WRONG WITH THE AIR AND PLANTS?
BUT IT'S LIKE SITTING WITH A GHOST.
ARE YOU HERE TO DO US HARM? CAN WE TRADE?
I THINK YOU HAVE MUCH TO OFFER IN EXCHANGE.
BUT IF YOU DON'T TALK TO ME, YOUR USEFULNESS WILL BE QUESTIONED, AND YOUR FATE WILL PASS OUT OF MY HANDS.
I'VE SPENT MY WHOLE LIFE NOT FEELING SAFE.
FLEEING FROM PLACE TO PLACE, TRYING TO OUTRUN THE TERRIBLE WORLD.
THAT SOUNDS FAMILIAR.
THIS IS NOT MY REALITY. I'VE BEEN PULLED INTO ANOTHER WORLD.
I HAVE TO BE OUT THERE TO SEE IF IT'S REAL.
THEN I'LL TALK.
FAIR ENOUGH. I'LL MAKE ARRANGEMENTS.
BUT YOU MIGHT NOT LIKE THE PLAN.

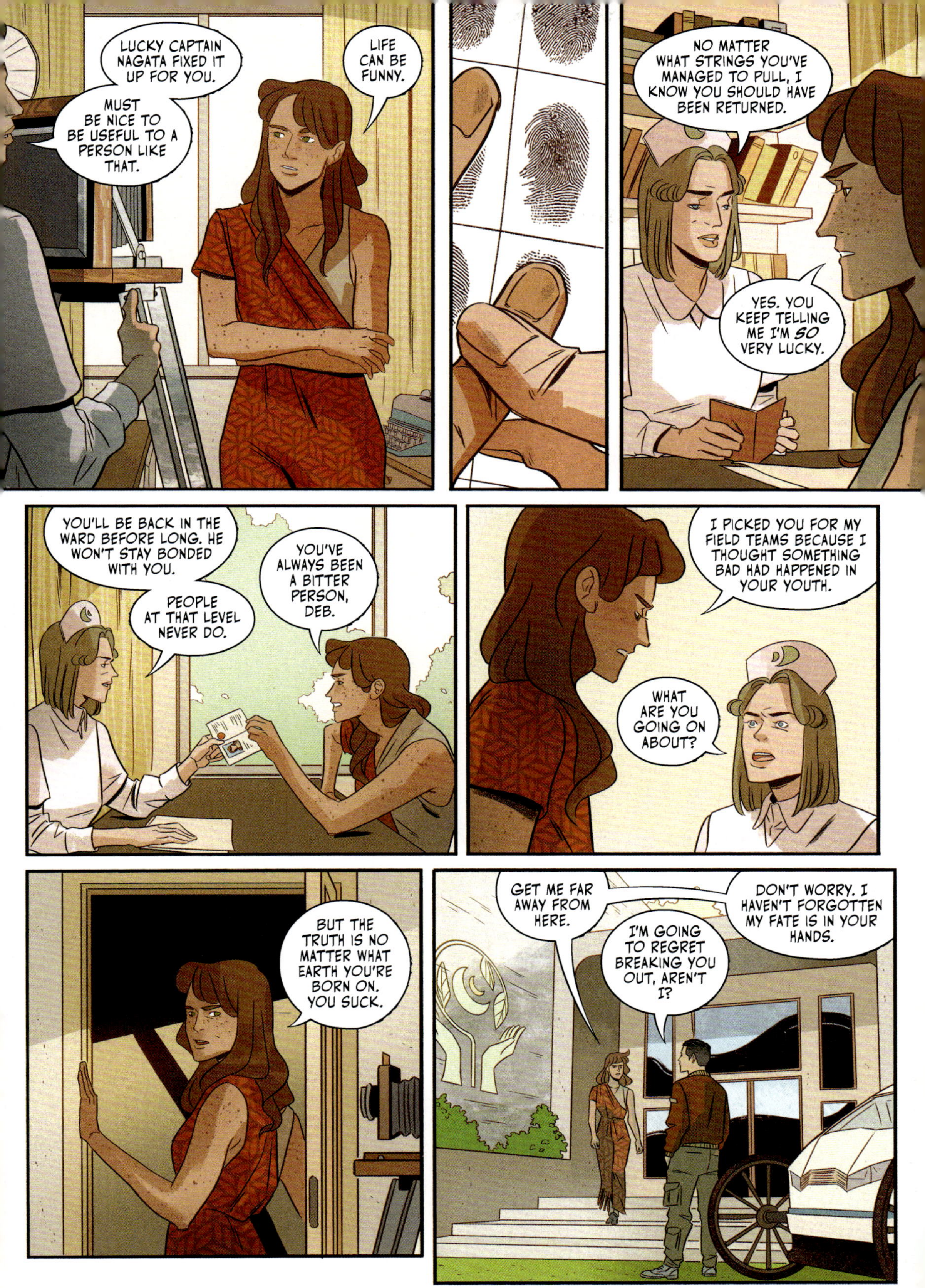
LUCKY CAPTAIN NAGATA FIXED IT UP FOR YOU.
MUST BE NICE TO BE USEFUL TO A PERSON LIKE THAT.
LIFE CAN BE FUNNY.
NO MATTER WHAT STRINGS YOU'VE MANAGED TO PULL, I KNOW YOU SHOULD HAVE BEEN RETURNED.
YES. YOU KEEP TELLING ME I'M *SO* VERY LUCKY.
YOU'LL BE BACK IN THE WARD BEFORE LONG. HE WON'T STAY BONDED WITH YOU.
PEOPLE AT THAT LEVEL NEVER DO.
YOU'VE ALWAYS BEEN A BITTER PERSON, DEB.
I PICKED YOU FOR MY FIELD TEAMS BECAUSE I THOUGHT SOMETHING BAD HAD HAPPENED IN YOUR YOUTH.
WHAT ARE YOU GOING ON ABOUT?
BUT THE TRUTH IS NO MATTER WHAT EARTH YOU'RE BORN ON. YOU SUCK.
GET ME FAR AWAY FROM HERE.
DON'T WORRY. I HAVEN'T FORGOTTEN MY FATE IS IN YOUR HANDS.
I'M GOING TO REGRET BREAKING YOU OUT, AREN'T I?

Dear Ramona, the storms here have been battering us hard.
It's been two weeks and no ships have come to fuel up on their long voyages.
I fear they are lost.
WE'RE SITTING ON ALL THIS POWER, AND WE CAN'T GET IT TO SHORE.
AT THIS RATE WE'LL HAVE TO SHOOT IT BACK OUT TO SEA. WHAT A WASTE.
IMAGINE THE GOOD IT WOULD DO IF WE COULD GET IT TO LAND.
YOU COULD HELP ME COME UP WITH A SOLUTION TO SALVAGE THE POWER INSTEAD OF JUST WHITTLING AWAY.
WHY? IN A MILLION YEARS OUR MINOR MOON WILL CRASH INTO THE MAJOR ONE AND THE OCEANS WILL SETTLE.
WE CAN MEASURE ALL WE WANT, BUT THAT'S WHAT'S AFFECTING THE WAVES, THE STORMS, THE FLOODING, THE LAND SHRINKAGE.
IT'S THE MOONS.
UNLESS--

UNLESS WHAT?
I SEE YOU SCRIBBLING AWAY IN YOUR NOTEBOOK. MUTTERING ON ABOUT SOMETHING.
YOU HAVE A *THEORY.*
I'M TRYING TO WORK OUT A WAY OFF THIS FACILITY. I'M NOT GOING TO BE STUCK HERE FOREVER LIKE YOU.
NO. IT'S MORE THAN THAT.
ONE THING I KNOW ABOUT THIS PLACE. GIVES YOU TIME TO THINK.
ABOUT LIFE. ABOUT THE NATURE OF THE UNIVERSE.
NO ONE OUT HERE CARES IF YOUR THOUGHTS ARE OF USE TO THEM. YOU'LL COME TO TREASURE THAT.
I'LL ASK YOU TO *NOT* GO THROUGH MY THINGS.
I LIKE YOU, DR. REED.
YOU'RE MORE INTERESTING THAN THE OTHERS.
MY ADVICE? FORGET THIS WORK AND DO YOUR OWN.
THAT'S WHAT I DO. MAYBE WE'LL EVEN WORK TOGETHER.
UNLIKELY.
Dr. Parnak just sits in the corner. He's useless.
Ramona, tell me. Have you found anything about my metal beast?

YOU'RE LUCKY YOU LANDED ON LAURENTIA.
I CAN'T GET OVER THE LANDSCAPE.
VERDELINA HAS BEEN THRIVING AS A TOWN FOR OVER TWO HUNDRED YEARS. WE'RE STABLE.
I'VE SEEN YOU IN BIOLOGY CLASS, YOU MADE A GREAT POINT ABOUT URBAN GREEN SPACES.
ENGINEERING SUSTAINABLE CITIES IS A PASSION OF MINE.
I'VE BEEN HERE ON EXCHANGE SINCE MY TEEN YEARS. I TRAINED AS AN ENGINEER.
SO...EXCHANGE IS THE TRADE OF PEOPLE AND GOODS WITH OTHER ISLANDS TO AVOID WARS AND USEFULNESS IS CURRENCY.
WHAT'S YOUR THESIS TOPIC, EVAN?
SOIL FERTILITY. I'M TRYING TO FIND CHEMICAL WAYS TO REVIVE SOIL THAT HAS BEEN DECIMATED BY CLIMATE CRISIS.
EXCHANGE ASSURES WE ALL LIVE IN HARMONY. RESOURCES ARE POOLED AND TRADED. WE HELP EACH OTHER TO SURVIVE.
SOUNDS UTOPIC.
ISN'T THAT HOW IT IS WHERE YOU'RE FROM?
NO. THERE I'M ALWAYS AFRAID.
THERE'S NOTHING TO BE AFRAID OF HERE.

AT LONG LAST! I'VE KEPT THE FIRES BURNING HOPING FOR THIS DAY, BEN. I WORRIED YOU'D FORGOTTEN US.
I MISSED YOU TOO, JOPOUR.
AND I SEND PRIORITY RELIEF WHEN THE HIVE NEEDS REPAIR.
YOU DO. BUT THAT'S NOT THE SAME AS A VISIT. I HOPED YOU'D COME SOONER.
THIS IS MAEVE.
HELLO, MAEVE. WELCOME.
YOU KNOW I DON'T LIKE OWING FAVORS TO MADAME PREMIERE. SHE AND I SEE THE WORLD DIFFERENTLY.
I USE MY OWN CREDIT WHEN HELPING YOU. YOU HAVE NO DEBT.
GOOD TO HEAR. I'M PROUD YOU'VE DONE SO WELL.
I'VE NEVER KNOWN BEN TO MAKE ATTACHMENTS. LET ME LOOK AT YOU.
I'M A BOTANIST. I'M GOOD WITH PLANTS. HE SAID YOU GARDEN HERE.
THAT WE DO.
BEN CAME TO US AS A BOY. AND HE'S CLIMBED FAR.
HE IMPROVED THE HIVE'S STRUCTURES WHICH UPPED OUR ANNUAL YIELD.
I JUST WANT TO HELP THE WORLD, AND I DO IT BETTER ALONE THAN IN A HIVE.
HA, ALWAYS THE REBEL. NO PERSON IS AN ISLAND.

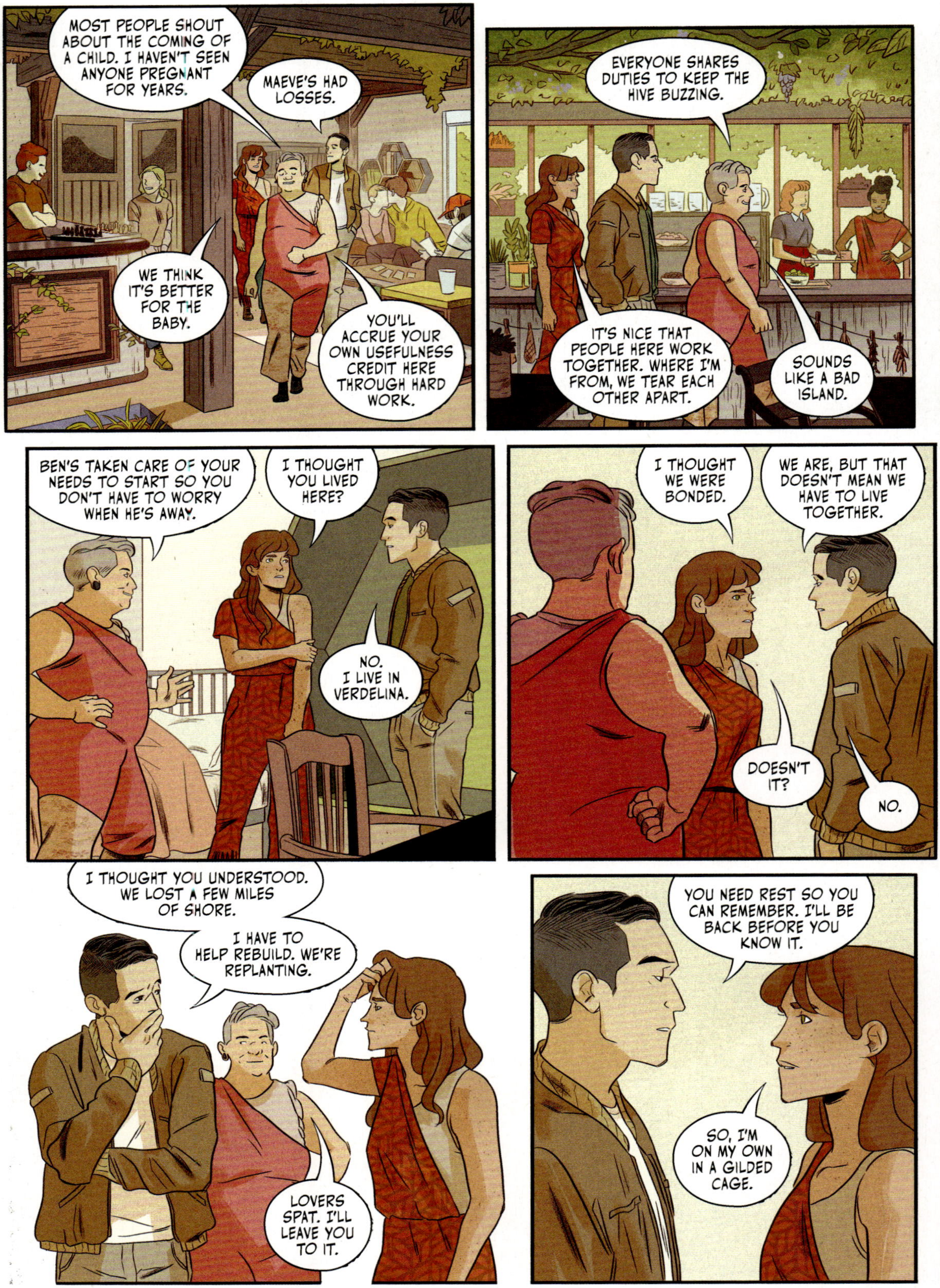
MOST PEOPLE SHOUT ABOUT THE COMING OF A CHILD. I HAVEN'T SEEN ANYONE PREGNANT FOR YEARS.
MAEVE'S HAD LOSSES.
WE THINK IT'S BETTER FOR THE BABY.
YOU'LL ACCRUE YOUR OWN USEFULNESS CREDIT HERE THROUGH HARD WORK.
EVERYONE SHARES DUTIES TO KEEP THE HIVE BUZZING.
IT'S NICE THAT PEOPLE HERE WORK TOGETHER. WHERE I'M FROM, WE TEAR EACH OTHER APART.
SOUNDS LIKE A BAD ISLAND.
BEN'S TAKEN CARE OF YOUR NEEDS TO START SO YOU DON'T HAVE TO WORRY WHEN HE'S AWAY.
I THOUGHT YOU LIVED HERE?
NO. I LIVE IN VERDELINA.
I THOUGHT WE WERE BONDED.
WE ARE, BUT THAT DOESN'T MEAN WE HAVE TO LIVE TOGETHER.
DOESN'T IT?
NO.
I THOUGHT YOU UNDERSTOOD. WE LOST A FEW MILES OF SHORE.
I HAVE TO HELP REBUILD. WE'RE REPLANTING.
LOVERS SPAT. I'LL LEAVE YOU TO IT.
YOU NEED REST SO YOU CAN REMEMBER. I'LL BE BACK BEFORE YOU KNOW IT.
SO, I'M ON MY OWN IN A GILDED CAGE.

YOU DO KNOW HOW TO USE ONE OF THESE! BEN WASN'T EXAGGERATING THIS TIME, WAS HE?
I FORAGE FOR WILD SEEDS TO HELP WITH DWINDLING BIODIVERSITY. I CROSSBREED PLANTS FOR TRAITS SO THAT THEY CAN SURVIVE THE ELEMENTS.
THAT *IS* USEFUL.
WAIT. DOES BEN EXAGGERATE?
NOT REALLY. HE JUST DOESN'T REVEAL.
THAT'S DIFFERENT.
I'M GLAD TO SEE YOU'RE NOT RUFFLED BY BEING DEMOTED TO A YOUTH HIVE. THE CITY HAS MORE COMFORTS.
I'VE SPENT MY WHOLE LIFE WAITING TO WORK IN A PLACE LIKE THIS.
GOOD, THEN I WON'T GO EASY ON YOU NO MATTER YOUR CONDITION.
OUR HIVE IS IN CHARGE OF FEEDING THIS WHOLE ZONE. IT'S ABOUT TWENTY SECTORS.
WE SUPPLY FOOD TO EVERYONE ON THE ISLAND. SURPLUS YIELD GOES TO EXCHANGE WITH OTHER ISLANDS.
SO, THERE'S NO FOOD INSECURITY.
AND HOW IS IT ORGANIZED? BEYOND EACH HEDGE IS A DIFFERENT MONO-CROP?
HOLY FUCK.
I NEVER IN MY WILDEST DREAMS THOUGHT I'D SEE THIS KIND OF THING.

YOU'RE PRACTICING PERMACULTURE. YOU DON'T STRESS THE SOIL.
WHO WOULD DO IT ANY OTHER WAY?
YOU'D BE SURPRISED.
THAT'S SILLY. A PLANT PROTECTS A PLANT PROTECTS A BIRD PROTECTS A BEE AND SO ON.
THIS COULD BE A WORLD TO HAVE A CHILD IN.
A WORLD THAT HAS A FUTURE.
THANK YOU, JOPOUR. I KNOW JUST HOW I CAN BE OF USE.
I COULD ALMOST BE HAPPY HERE.

3.

You should know that while
we didn't always see eye to eye,
we loved each other very much.

And we love you.

She was infuriating in the way
that she felt everything.

She couldn't do it alone.
None of us can.

I loved that about her,
and I see it in you.

Four Months Later
IF ONLY WE COULD GET THESE SEEDS BACK HOME.
IF WE COULD EVER GET THERE. BACK TO EVAN.
CLANG CLANG CLANG
HE'D FREAK OUT. ABOUT THIS IDYLLIC PLACE. ABOUT YOU.
CLANG CLANG CLANG
GETTING HOME SEEMS IMPOSSIBLE. I WON'T GIVE UP TRYING, BUT...
MAYBE WE COULD BE HAPPY HERE.
CLANG
CLANG CLANG
THE TECH HERE IS DIFFERENT. THEY'RE 150 YEARS BEHIND US IN SOME WAYS AND 150 AHEAD IN OTHERS.
IT STILL FEELS UNREAL!
CLANG CLANG CLANG
HONESTLY, I DON'T KNOW IF I WANT TO GO BACK, JELLYBEAN. IT'S WORSE THERE.
MAEVE! COME QUICK!
CLANG CLANG CLANG

DIDN'T YOU HEAR THE BELLS? WE HAVE TO GET TO SHELTER!
I DIDN'T KNOW WHAT THEY MEANT. I THOUGHT IT WAS FOR LUNCH OR A SPIRITUAL SERVICE.
BUT IT'S BEEN HARD TO LEARN THE WAYS OF A NEW WORLD.
HANG ON!
WOAH!
HERE LIFE IS TREACHEROUS IN A DIFFERENT WAY.
UGH! JOPOUR-- HELP!
I'LL COME DOWN AND GET YOU.
WHICH BRING ME DIFFERENT SORTS OF NIGHTMARES.

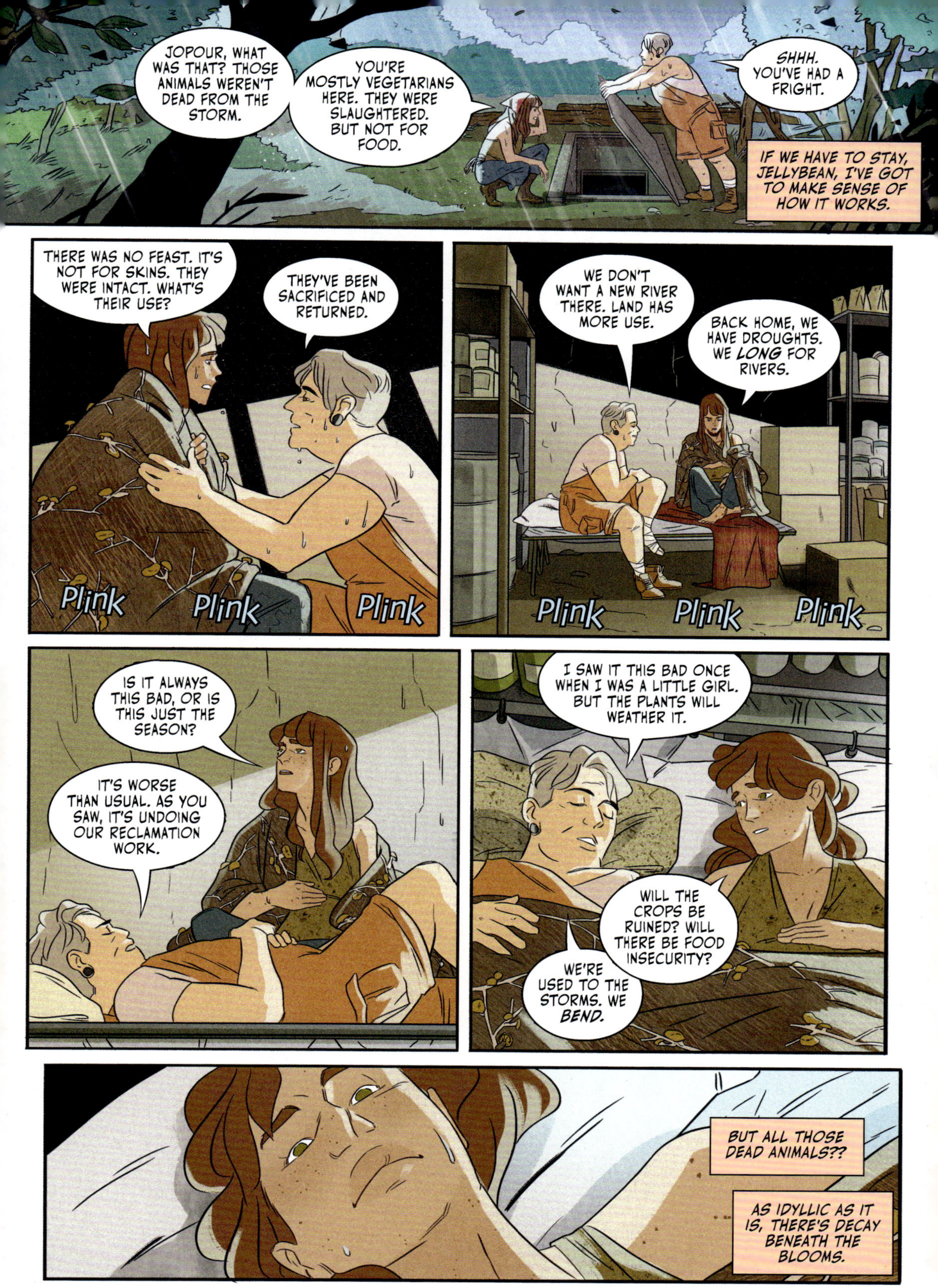
JOPOUR, WHAT WAS THAT? THOSE ANIMALS WEREN'T DEAD FROM THE STORM.
YOU'RE MOSTLY VEGETARIANS HERE. THEY WERE SLAUGHTERED. BUT NOT FOR FOOD.
SHHH. YOU'VE HAD A FRIGHT.
IF WE HAVE TO STAY, JELLYBEAN, I'VE GOT TO MAKE SENSE OF HOW IT WORKS.
THERE WAS NO FEAST. IT'S NOT FOR SKINS. THEY WERE INTACT. WHAT'S THEIR USE?
THEY'VE BEEN SACRIFICED AND RETURNED.
Plink Plink Plink
WE DON'T WANT A NEW RIVER THERE. LAND HAS MORE USE.
BACK HOME, WE HAVE DROUGHTS. WE LONG FOR RIVERS.
Plink Plink Plink
IS IT ALWAYS THIS BAD, OR IS THIS JUST THE SEASON?
IT'S WORSE THAN USUAL. AS YOU SAW, IT'S UNDOING OUR RECLAMATION WORK.
I SAW IT THIS BAD ONCE WHEN I WAS A LITTLE GIRL. BUT THE PLANTS WILL WEATHER IT.
WILL THE CROPS BE RUINED? WILL THERE BE FOOD INSECURITY?
WE'RE USED TO THE STORMS. WE BEND.
BUT ALL THOSE DEAD ANIMALS??
AS IDYLLIC AS IT IS, THERE'S DECAY BENEATH THE BLOOMS.

WEEOO WEEOOO WEEOO
Dear Ramona, we almost lost the station today.
I am sure that this unprecedented storm cycle is connected with the tear I saw in the sky.
WEEOO WEEOO WEEOOO
I hope it's easier to ride out in the city.
ALL HANDS-ON DECK.
WEEOO WEEOO WEEOOO
Here, the ocean acts as though it wants to throw us off the planet.

MORE SALT ON ME AND THIS DECK THAN THERE'S LEFT IN THE OCEAN.
IT'S A DRAMATIC WATER LEVEL RISE, THAT'S FOR SURE.
BUT IT'S NOT MOON WOBBLE YET.
The waters are too rough to sail, and we've heard more islands and transports have been called back to the depths.
WE'LL HAVE TO RAISE THE FACILITY OR WE'RE DEAD IN THE WAVES.
RAISING NOW.
THOSE BIRDS HAVE BEEN CIRCLING FOR HOURS. THEY LOOK *DISORIENTED.*
WARBLERS. FUNNY, SEEING THEM HERE. THEY'RE WAY OFF COURSE.
Like the birds, the boats are lost at sea.
WHAT THE...?
DR. REED. *COME.*
DR. PARNAK, IF WE DON'T GET THIS PLACE RUNNING AGAIN, WE'LL BE DEEMED USELESS.
Out here it's not living, it's surviving.
DR. PARNAK!
Will I ever see you again, my love?

SINCE YOU'VE ARRIVED, I'VE BEEN THINKING ABOUT RESEARCH FROM MY YOUTH THAT I'D PUT ASIDE.
Ramona, there are universal mysteries to solve, and I can't do it from here.
THERE MIGHT BE A CONNECTION BETWEEN THAT SECRET WORK YOU DO AND AN OLD THEORY OF MINE.
NOT LIKELY.
Have you had any luck researching my beast?
I SAW SOMETHING WHEN I WAS YOUNG.
SUNSPOTS? THEY HAPPEN ALL THE TIME.
THAT THEY DO. THERE ARE CYCLES EVERYWHERE. LIKE OUR MOONS THAT WOBBLE EVERY 18 YEARS.
THERE ARE INVISIBLE FORCES IN THE UNIVERSE WE HAVE YET TO UNDERSTAND.
I SAW THE SKY OPEN AS THOUGH A GREAT TRANSFER OF ENERGY...
AN ACTION AND A REACTION...
DR. PARNAK, YOU MAY BE ONTO SOMETHING.
AND IT ALL STARTED WHEN I SAW THIS THING.
MAYBE A DOOR OPENS TO OTHER WORLDS. MAYBE IT'S OPENING AGAIN.

STILL THERE. STABLE.
I WONDER IF...
SHIT. SMALLER BUT *STRONGER.*
WHUUUM WHUUUM
FIGURE IT OUT FIRST. FIND WHAT USE IT MIGHT HAVE. THEN TAKE ADVANTAGE.
NO ENTRY
CAPTAIN NAGATA. HOP IN. I'LL TAKE YOU TO THE SITE.
WE NEED TO TALK.

I HEAR YOU HAVE A PREGNANT BOND MATE NOW. WELL DONE.
SHE'S UNDER OUR PROTECTION NOW.
SHE'S FAR FROM HOME. ALONE.
I HAD A CHILD ONCE. A SWEET THING, BUT SADLY IT FAILED TO THRIVE.
NOW I TAKE COMFORT IN KNOWING LAURENTIA AND ITS PEOPLE WILL PROSPER UNDER MY CARE.
OUR PROGRESS WITH NEW TECHNOLOGIES IS NOT SOMETHING I WANT TO SHARE WITH OTHER ISLANDS.
UNDERSTOOD. STOCKPILE RESOURCES. CONTROL SUPPLY. EVERYTHING FLOWS FROM US.
I'M GLAD YOU'VE ABSORBED MY IDEAS OF NEW ECONOMICS, BEN.
THERE WILL BE RESISTANCE TO THIS NEW WAY. THE SELF OVER THE WHOLE.
WHICH IS WHY YOU NEED TO NIP IT IN THE BUD.
EVEN IF THAT MEANS VIOLENCE.

HERE I AM FACE TO FACE WITH EVERYTHING WE ALL LOST ON EARTH. IT'S BITTERSWEET.
YET, I WANT TO GO HOME, JELLYBEAN. HOME IS WHAT YOU KNOW.
HERE THEY FOLLOW THE PHILOSOPHY OF A SUSTAINABLE WAY OF LIFE IN A PEACEFUL, COMMUNAL WAY...
LIFE BURSTS EVERYWHERE. THERE'S... KINDNESS.
YET ON EVERY WALK, I LOOK FOR THAT PLACE WHERE I ARRIVED, HOPING THERE'S A WAY BACK.
I KNOW WHAT I'VE FOUND HERE COULD BE USEFUL BACK HOME.
HA! I BET I COULD EVEN WORK WITH EVAN.
HEY THERE. YOU'RE SEEDING THE MUSHROOM SPORES, AREN'T YOU?
IT'S ALMOST LAND DAY. MY TURN TO FEED THE TREE.
THERE ARE FACES OF PEOPLE I KNOW EVERY-WHERE, BUT I DO NOT KNOW THEM.
THIS MAN LOOKS LIKE MR. BEAUDRY, THE OLD MAIL CARRIER.
I WOULDN'T MIND A TASTE OF LIFE'S SWEETNESS BEFORE MY WORK IS DONE.
SHALL WE TRADE?
THEY MUST BE LOOKING FOR ME. THOSE SCIENTISTS SAW ME BEING PULLED AWAY. EVAN WOULDN'T GIVE UP.
BACK HOME, JELLYBEAN, WE HAVE GO BAGS IN CASE THERE'S A NEED TO EVACUATE.
I COULD DO THE SAME HERE WITH SEEDS, JUST IN CASE A CRACK THROUGH SPACE AROSE AGAIN.

TELL ME *EVERYTHING,* DR. PARNAK.
IT WAS FIFTY YEARS AGO, WHEN I WAS ON EXCHANGE ON AN ISLAND IN THE DEEP BLUE THAT IS NOW LONG GONE. HAMOU--BEAUTIFUL PLACE.
THERE WERE LARGE SUNSPOTS, LIKE THERE WERE TODAY. AND THEN A FLASH OF BRIGHT LIGHT.
"I MOVED MY EYE AWAY FROM THE POLARIZED LENS.
"THAT'S WHEN I SAW IT. THIS BEAST FLYING OUT OF A RIP IN THE SKY.
"BUT I REALIZED IT WASN'T ORGANIC, IT WAS A *MACHINE.*
"AND IT LET SOMETHING LOOSE FROM ITS BELLY.
"DAY BECAME BRIGHTER AND THE BEAST FELL THROUGH THE CLOUDS. IT WENT DOWN AT AN ATOLL NOT FAR AWAY.
"DEAD FISH WASHED ASHORE FOR DAYS."
IT WAS YEARS BEFORE I COULD PINPOINT THE PLACE. BUT I FINALLY DID.
IT'S WHY I ACCEPTED THE WAVES FACILITY AS MY EXILE.

THAT'S WHAT I SAW! A MECHANICAL BEAST. A TEAR IN THE SKY. BUT IT SNAPPED SHUT.
I'VE POURED THROUGH THE ARCHIVES. MAGNETIC STORMS IN THE PAST ARE CITED--
--BUT NO MENTION OF THESE MACHINES.
ONLY MY OBSERVATIONS FROM FIFTY YEARS AGO. I WAS LAUGHED OUT OF THE ACADEMY.
THE AURORAS WERE SO BRIGHT THAT NIGHT YOU WOULD THINK IT WAS DAYTIME.
COME, THERE'S SOMETHING YOU SHOULD SEE.
HOW WERE THE STORMS?
BAD FOR MONTHS. AND THEN BACK TO NORMAL. UNTIL NOW.
I FOUND SOMEONE IN THE WRECKAGE BACK THEN.
BURNT TO DEATH LIKE HE'D BEEN DANCING WITH THE SUN.
THE WRECK, THE PHENOMENON, ALL ARE VITAL THINGS TO BE STUDIED, I THINK.
THEY WON'T IGNORE US NOW. SOMETHING ELSE IS OUT THERE. KNOWING THAT IS OF *USE.*
ASSUMING THEY KNEW USE FROM THEIR ASSES.

IS THIS THE BEAST THAT YOU SAW?
NO. WHAT I SAW WAS SLEEKER. SMALLER. LIKE AN OVERGROWN INSECT.
IS IT POSSIBLE THAT SOMEONE CAME OVER THIS TIME, MORE THAN ONE, PERHAPS? AND ARE STILL ALIVE?
IF IT *IS* A DOOR BETWEEN WORLDS, YES. BUT WHO? WHERE?
I HAVE THOSE IMPACT COORDINATES. I SAW AN ORGANIC BLOB ENTER.
WHOEVER THESE VISITORS ARE, THEY'RE TECHNOLOGICALLY MORE ADVANCED THAN US.
I'D LOVE TO ASK THEM. EXCHANGE IDEAS. WHY OUR PLANET, AND WHY NOW?
ARE THEY A THREAT, I WONDER? OR PERHAPS...OUR SALVATION?
I ALWAYS BELIEVED THERE WERE OTHER WORLDS.
LET'S HEAD TO THE IMPACT SITE. ANSWERS *MUST* BE THERE.
THEN WITH YOUR WORK TO BACK UP MINE, THEY'VE *GOT* TO LISTEN.

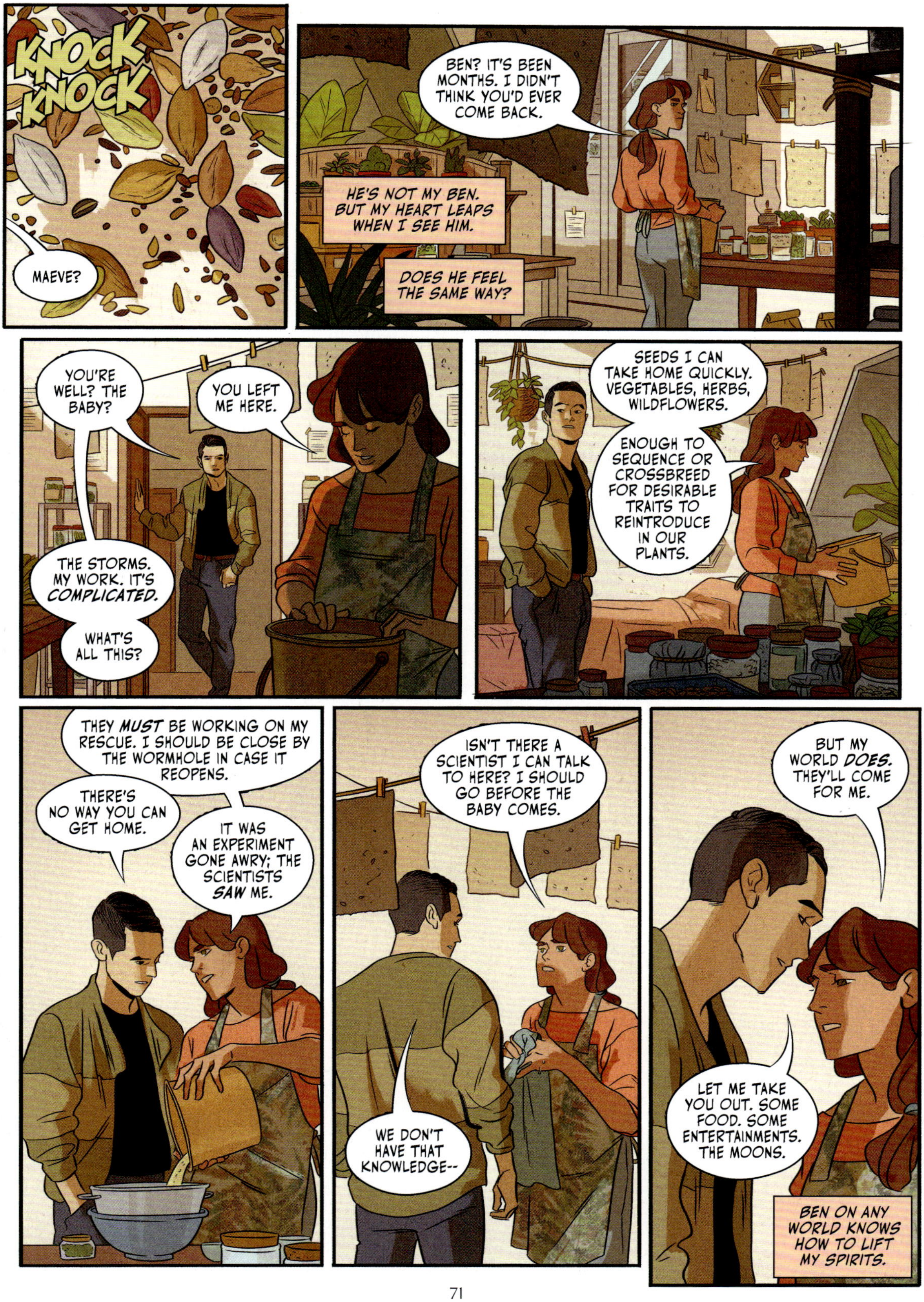
KNOCK KNOCK
MAEVE?
BEN? IT'S BEEN MONTHS. I DIDN'T THINK YOU'D EVER COME BACK.
HE'S NOT MY BEN. BUT MY HEART LEAPS WHEN I SEE HIM.
DOES HE FEEL THE SAME WAY?
YOU'RE WELL? THE BABY?
YOU LEFT ME HERE.
THE STORMS. MY WORK. IT'S COMPLICATED.
WHAT'S ALL THIS?
SEEDS I CAN TAKE HOME QUICKLY. VEGETABLES, HERBS, WILDFLOWERS.
ENOUGH TO SEQUENCE OR CROSSBREED FOR DESIRABLE TRAITS TO REINTRODUCE IN OUR PLANTS.
THEY MUST BE WORKING ON MY RESCUE. I SHOULD BE CLOSE BY THE WORMHOLE IN CASE IT REOPENS.
THERE'S NO WAY YOU CAN GET HOME.
IT WAS AN EXPERIMENT GONE AWRY; THE SCIENTISTS SAW ME.
ISN'T THERE A SCIENTIST I CAN TALK TO HERE? I SHOULD GO BEFORE THE BABY COMES.
WE DON'T HAVE THAT KNOWLEDGE--
BUT MY WORLD DOES. THEY'LL COME FOR ME.
LET ME TAKE YOU OUT. SOME FOOD. SOME ENTERTAINMENTS. THE MOONS.
BEN ON ANY WORLD KNOWS HOW TO LIFT MY SPIRITS.

DO YOU LIKE IT?
WOW.
"The two siblings having caught sight of Sol, fell in love and did not reveal that their hearts had been captured by his orbit."
I do not like the look of him. (But the attraction is so strong.)
"Sol asked the siblings to dance with him in the sky, but both refused out of love for each other."
I want to but could never leave my sister.
My love for you is too strong, brother.
"Thinking he was rejected by the cold-hearted siblings, Sol gave his heart to Mother Earth, who bloomed at his warmth."

Sol is too bright. (But I cannot look away.)
We can make life difficult for every child she bears him.
Until she has nothing left but an ocean of her tears.
My children's children will fill the land and dry my eyes.

OUR ONE MOON IS LIKE THE LARGER MOON HERE, BUT IT'S FEMALE.
ONLY ONE MOON? I CAN'T IMAGINE IT.
SHE DRIVES A CHARIOT ACROSS THE SKY. OR LIVES IN THE MOON. SHE'S ALONE. OR HAS A RABBIT.
WE ARE TESTED BY THE MOON SIBLINGS. THEY BATTER US BY FORCES BEYOND OUR CONTROL.
WE ALL MAKE UP STORIES TO MAKE SENSE OF THE WORLD. LIKE THE ONE I'M TELLING YOU NOW.
THE MOON AFFECTS OUR TIDES, AND WOMEN'S COURSES AS WELL. BUT I THINK MORE SO HERE.
OUR NUMBERS DIMINISH JUST AS OUR LAND DOES.
I'LL NEVER GET USED TO EATING INSECTS.
WHAT DO YOU EAT AT HOME?
COWS. CHICKENS. GOATS. LAMBS.
SOUNDS HORRIBLE.
MY BEN LOVED A GOOD MEAT BURGER, THOUGH.
IT'S SO STRINGY, I ALWAYS THINK IT WILL BE CRUNCHY.
IT'S DELICIOUS.
WE HAVE A MOONBASE. RIGHT NEAR THAT BIG CRATER. SIX ASTRONAUTS LIVING THERE.
HUMANS LIVING ON THE MOON? HOW?
WE FLY THERE. WE FLY EVERYWHERE. THOUGH IT'S DAMAGED US.

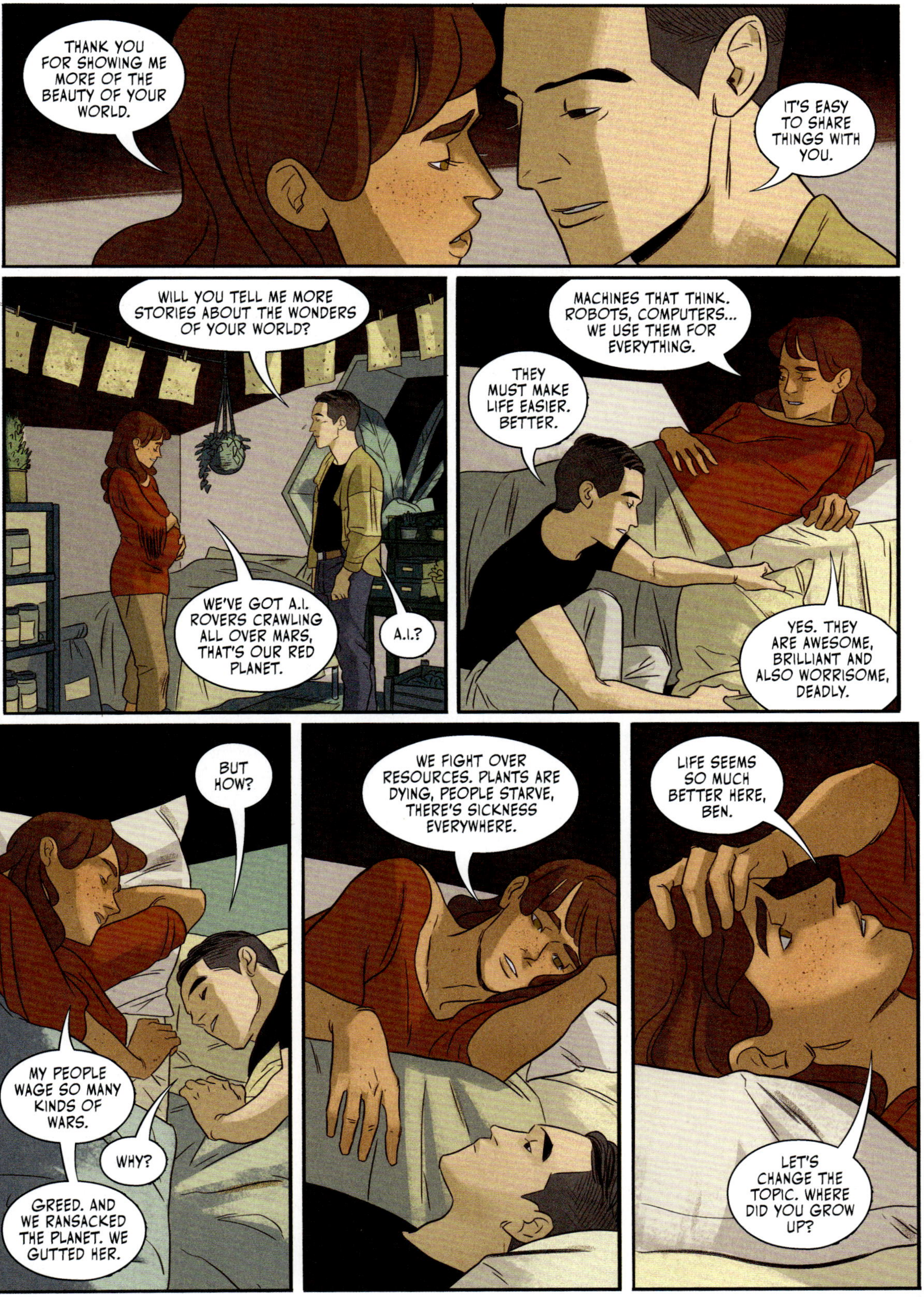
THANK YOU FOR SHOWING ME MORE OF THE BEAUTY OF YOUR WORLD.
IT'S EASY TO SHARE THINGS WITH YOU.
WILL YOU TELL ME MORE STORIES ABOUT THE WONDERS OF YOUR WORLD?
WE'VE GOT A.I. ROVERS CRAWLING ALL OVER MARS, THAT'S OUR RED PLANET.
A.I.?
MACHINES THAT THINK. ROBOTS, COMPUTERS... WE USE THEM FOR EVERYTHING.
THEY MUST MAKE LIFE EASIER. BETTER.
YES. THEY ARE AWESOME, BRILLIANT AND ALSO WORRISOME, DEADLY.
BUT HOW?
MY PEOPLE WAGE SO MANY KINDS OF WARS.
WHY?
GREED. AND WE RANSACKED THE PLANET. WE GUTTED HER.
WE FIGHT OVER RESOURCES. PLANTS ARE DYING, PEOPLE STARVE, THERE'S SICKNESS EVERYWHERE.
LIFE SEEMS SO MUCH BETTER HERE, BEN.
LET'S CHANGE THE TOPIC. WHERE DID YOU GROW UP?

"I GREW UP ON YARMAN. I WAS BROUGHT UP WITH THE REST OF THE CHILDREN IN GROUP CRÈCHE.
"OUR APTITUDES WERE TESTED. I SCORED HIGH IN MATH. I WAS EXCHANGED TO ANOTHER ISLAND WITH CHILDREN WHO HAD SKILLS MY ISLAND LACKED.
"EXCHANGE MINIMIZES VIOLENCE BETWEEN THE ISLANDS. WE TRADE THINKERS, LABORERS, CARETAKERS BALANCING THE KIND OF POPULATION THAT EACH ISLAND NEEDS TO THRIVE.
"IT WAS A HAPPY TIME. I MOVED FROM ISLAND TO ISLAND, WORKING AS AN APPRENTICE BUILDER, HONING MY ENGINEERING SKILL. I WAS SO USEFUL THAT I WAS EXCHANGED TO LAURENTIA.
"MOST OF THOSE ISLANDS ARE GONE. I LEARNED YOUNG TO MAKE NO ATTACHMENTS.
"UNTIL YOU, JOPOUR IS THE ONLY PERSON I'VE EVER CARED FOR. BUT THEY DON'T APPROVE OF MY LIFE CHOICES.
"I BECAME COMMITTED TO ONE THING: GROWING THE LAND.
"I JOINED THE NEW GUARD TO FOCUS ON CIVIL PROJECTS TO STRENGTHEN OUR INFRASTRUCTURE."
THE FLOOR MUST BE VERY UNCOMFORT-ABLE, BEN.
JOIN ME.

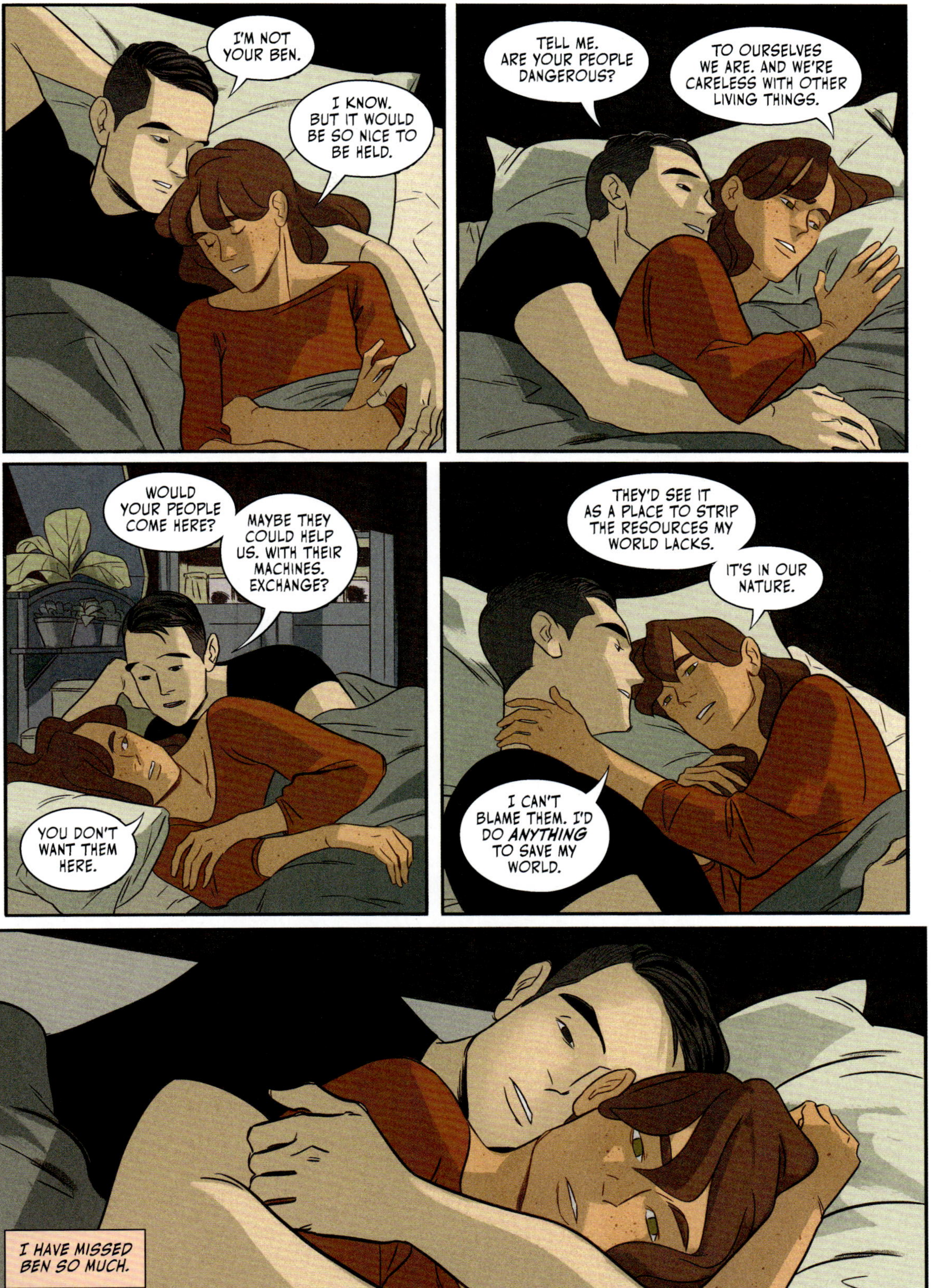
I'M NOT YOUR BEN.
I KNOW. BUT IT WOULD BE SO NICE TO BE HELD.
TELL ME. ARE YOUR PEOPLE DANGEROUS?
TO OURSELVES WE ARE. AND WE'RE CARELESS WITH OTHER LIVING THINGS.
WOULD YOUR PEOPLE COME HERE?
MAYBE THEY COULD HELP US. WITH THEIR MACHINES. EXCHANGE?
YOU DON'T WANT THEM HERE.
THEY'D SEE IT AS A PLACE TO STRIP THE RESOURCES MY WORLD LACKS.
IT'S IN OUR NATURE.
I CAN'T BLAME THEM. I'D DO *ANYTHING* TO SAVE MY WORLD.
I HAVE MISSED BEN SO MUCH.

CHIRP CHIRP
MORNING, JOPOUR.
HAVE YOU SEEN, BEN? HE WASN'T THERE WHEN I WOKE UP.
HE LEFT. HE'S ALWAYS GOT SOMETHING MORE IMPORTANT TO DO. FOR THE PREMIERE.
BEN'S LOST A LOT, NO KIN, NO ISLAND, FRIENDS DEAD. ALL SWALLOWED UP BY THE OCEAN. HE WAS SLOW TO CONNECT WITH OTHERS.
HIS FIRST LOVE IS THE LAND AND THAT MEANS LOYALTY TO MADAME PREMIERE.
I'M UNDER NO ILLUSIONS. OUR BOND ISN'T REAL, IT'S AN ARRANGEMENT.
THERE YOU ARE LITTLE ONES.
HELP ME GATHER BRANCHES TO MAKE A HABITAT NOW THAT THE WEATHER'S FINALLY HOLDING.
YOU DON'T APPROVE OF BEN'S CHOICES?
HE'S THE CHILD I NEVER HAD. I'M HARD ON HIM.
HOW *DO* FAMILIES WORK HERE, JOPOUR?
NO MATTER WHERE I LOOK. I DON'T SEE THEM. NOT HERE, NOT IN THE CITY.
WHO?
THE CHILDREN? WHERE ARE THEY?

CHILDREN ARE RARE.
NOT EVERY FEMALE HAS A CYCLE.
GROW LEARN
SO, YOU SEPARATE THE CHILDREN. WHAT ABOUT THEIR MENTAL DEVELOPMENT?
SOME ISLANDS FORM FAMILY UNITS BECAUSE THEIR NUMBERS ARE SMALL.
HERE AT THE CRÈCHE, CHILDREN ARE CARED FOR AND LOVED AND GUIDED TO THEIR MOST USEFUL PATH.
IT'S EASIER ON SOCIETY.
EVERYONE AND EVERYTHING IS USEFUL.
SHARE TO CARE = CARE TO SHARE
WHAT HAPPENS WHEN A PERSON ISN'T USEFUL?
THERE ARE MANY STAGES BEFORE THAT HAPPENS.
BUT *WHAT* HAPPENS?
THIS IS MY ISLAND NOW

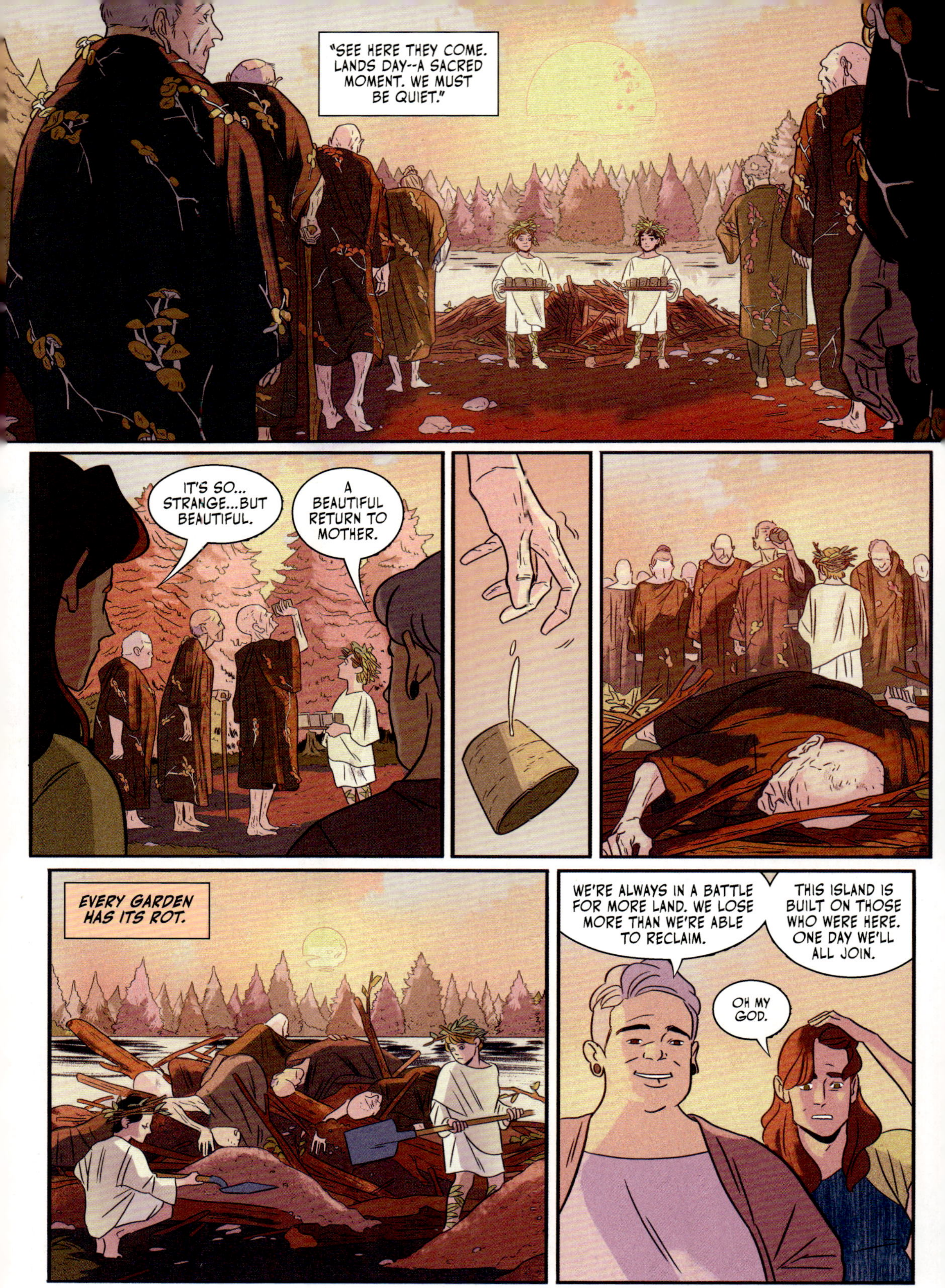
"SEE HERE THEY COME. LANDS DAY--A SACRED MOMENT. WE MUST BE QUIET."
IT'S SO... STRANGE...BUT BEAUTIFUL.
A BEAUTIFUL RETURN TO MOTHER.
EVERY GARDEN HAS ITS ROT.
WE'RE ALWAYS IN A BATTLE FOR MORE LAND. WE LOSE MORE THAN WE'RE ABLE TO RECLAIM.
THIS ISLAND IS BUILT ON THOSE WHO WERE HERE. ONE DAY WE'LL ALL JOIN.
OH MY GOD.

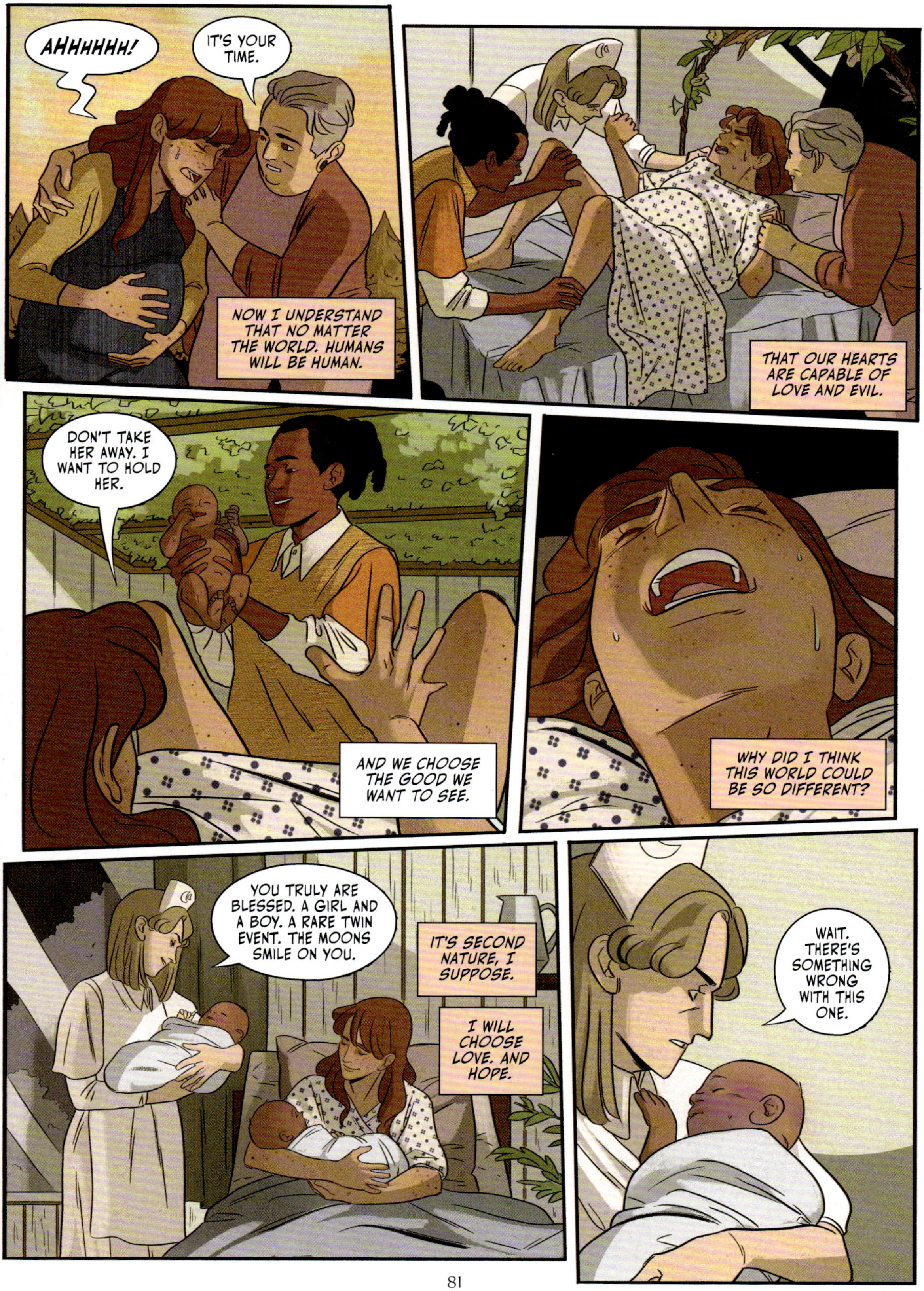
AHHHHHH!
IT'S YOUR TIME.
NOW I UNDERSTAND THAT NO MATTER THE WORLD. HUMANS WILL BE HUMAN.
THAT OUR HEARTS ARE CAPABLE OF LOVE AND EVIL.
DON'T TAKE HER AWAY. I WANT TO HOLD HER.
AND WE CHOOSE THE GOOD WE WANT TO SEE.
WHY DID I THINK THIS WORLD COULD BE SO DIFFERENT?
YOU TRULY ARE BLESSED. A GIRL AND A BOY. A RARE TWIN EVENT. THE MOONS SMILE ON YOU.
IT'S SECOND NATURE, I SUPPOSE.
I WILL CHOOSE LOVE. AND HOPE.
WAIT. THERE'S SOMETHING WRONG WITH THIS ONE.

4.

She came into my life
unexpectedly, as you did.

Though I only knew her briefly,
she had the answers for things
that I couldn't bring back.

She had the ideas and the
lived experience to know how
to make things better.

So did I.

We both did what we had to do.

OBSERVATION 30th moon, Fourth Day, Cycle 55 Rough crossing. Compass failure. Navigated by stars. Encountered zero ships. Midday landfall.
Prime event localized. Effects felt throughout the island and ocean.
THERE.
STUNNING.
MAGNETICS GOING HAYWIRE. WHATEVER THIS IS, IT'S BIG. AN UNPRECEDENTED EVENT.
EVERYTHING PULLS TOWARDS THAT AREA AHEAD. NOTICE THE VEGETATION. INFECTION?
PERHAPS. PUSH FORWARD. CAREFULLY.
LOOK--IT'S PULSING. THINGS...MATTER... PARTICLES...ARE FLOWING TO IT.
COULD BE BLEED FROM ONE WORLD TO THE OTHER? LOOKS LIKE THERE'S NO COHESION.
STRIKE OFF INVASION HYPOTHESES. NOTHING BIG COULD GET THROUGH THAT.
THE MASS OF AN OBJECT TRANSFERRING THROUGH THE PORTAL MUST BE RELATIVE TO THE AMOUNT OF ENERGY UNLEASHED.
SO, A POWERFUL FORCE INCITED IT. LIKE THE SUN...THOSE SUNSPOTS ARE HUGE. FLARES CAN AFFECT US HERE...
NOW YOU'RE THINKING.

IT'S PROBABLY THE REASON FOR THESE MAGNETIC STORMS.
THE MOONS COULD ALSO BE AFFECTED BY THE OTHER WORLD'S PULL, SPELLING EVENTUAL DISASTER.
THE TEAR IN THE SKY THAT DAY A YEAR AGO...THE STARS IN MY VIEW WERE FOR A NIGHT TWO WEEKS FROM NOW.
I HAVE A WILD THEORY THAT TIME DOESN'T RUN THE SAME NEAR MASS.
IF THAT'S POSSIBLE THEN WE COULD REWRITE OUR WHOLE IDEA OF THE UNIVERSE.
THINGS WILL GET WORSE FOR OUR WORLD IF WE DON'T TRY TO SEAL IT.
NAVIGATION WILL BECOME IMPOSSIBLE. MAKING EVERY ISLAND ALONE.
TWO WEEKS, THEN. THAT'LL BE THE DAY TO COME BACK. WE'LL LAY LOW 'TIL THEN.
IT'S DIFFERENT THAN THE EVENT FROM MY YOUTH, BUT SIMILAR. ENERGY IS CAUSING A RIP.
NO ENTRY
ALL WE NEED IS PROOF. I'LL GET WORD TO MY BONDMATE RAMONA. SHE HAS THE EAR OF MADAME PREMIERE...
AND JUST LIKE THAT, I'M BACK. WE'LL BUILD A REAL LAB.
NATURALLY, I'LL BE IN CHARGE.
HA, WE'LL SEE ABOUT THAT. I'M NOT USELESS YET.
KEEP TELLING YOURSELF THAT, OLD MAN.
HEY!
SHIT.
HALT! YOU'RE IN VIOLATION. THIS AREA IS RESTRICTED. COME WITH ME.

WHAT'S THAT?
MOONS! WHAT IS HAPPENING? THE BIRDS DON'T SEEM TO EVEN KNOW HOW TO FLY!
MAEVE! GET INSIDE!
THE LIGHT LOOKS SO STRANGE ON ARLO.
YOU SEE IT TOO, RIGHT? I'M NOT DREAMING.

HE'S GOT A WEAK HEART, BUT ARLO LOOKS AS THOUGH HE'S FALLING APART.
LIKE BITS OF HIM ARE TRYING TO GO BACK TO MY WORLD.
STOP SAYING THINGS LIKE THAT. THEY'LL DEEM YOU READY FOR THE TREES.
I'VE GOTTA FIND BEN. THIS IS PROOF THAT HE WAS WRONG. I NEED TO LOOK IN THE FOREST WHERE I ARRIVED.
MAEVE... ENOUGH. YOU'RE HERE NOW. THIS IS YOUR HOME.
I WAS ON MY WORLD AND THEN PIECE BY PIECE I FELL APART AND MATERIALIZED HERE.
THAT'S THE STUFF OF STORIES. THE MOONS FALL IN LOVE WITH THE SUN...
BEN SAW. HE'LL TELL YOU. I'M NOT LYING.
IF IT'S HAPPENING AGAIN, I HAVE TO SEE IF THERE'S A WAY TO GET BACK HOME.
THERE ARE DOCTORS THERE WHO CAN CURE ARLO'S HEART.
BEN AND I HAVE GROWN CLOSER, BUT HE'S STILL CAGEY ABOUT WHERE HE GOES.
JOPOUR, I DON'T KNOW HOW TO REACH HIM.
I DO.
WHOA!
THIS IS WHERE BEN DISAPPEARS TO.
I TOLD YOU TO NEVER BRING HER HERE, JOPOUR!

IS *THIS* YOUR SECRET WORK?
YOU'RE DIGGING FOR COAL? HOW COULD YOU BE SO FUCKING STUPID?
I'M TRYING TO SAVE MY WORLD.
I SEE THIS EARTH HAS CHALLENGES AND MAJOR PROBLEMS, BUT THIS PATH IS NOT THE WAY TO SAVE YOUR PLANET.
WE LOSE THE LAND THAT WE TRY TO EXTEND TO THE TIDES AND STORMS. WE LOSE PEOPLE. WE LOSE INFRASTRUCTURE.
BUT WITH THIS FUEL...I'M INSPIRED TO THINK THESE RESOURCES CAN BE *WORLD* CHANGING.
WE BECAME DEPENDENT ON FOSSIL FUELS IN WAYS THAT WE'LL NEVER RECOVER FROM.
IN ONE HUNDRED YEARS, EVERYTHING YOU CHERISH, AND YOUR SUSTAINABLE WAY OF LIFE WILL BE GONE.
YOU WILL SUFFOCATE. PLANT LIFE WILL EXPIRE. PEOPLE WILL STARVE AND DIE.
WE'RE NOTHING LIKE YOUR WORLD.
YOU'RE *EXACTLY* LIKE MY WORLD. BECAUSE YOU'RE HUMAN, TOO.
WHY DID YOU COME TO SEE ME, MAEVE?
I NEED TO GET HOME.
AS MUCH AS IT'S AWFUL THERE, OUR TECHNOLOGY CAN SAVE ARLO.

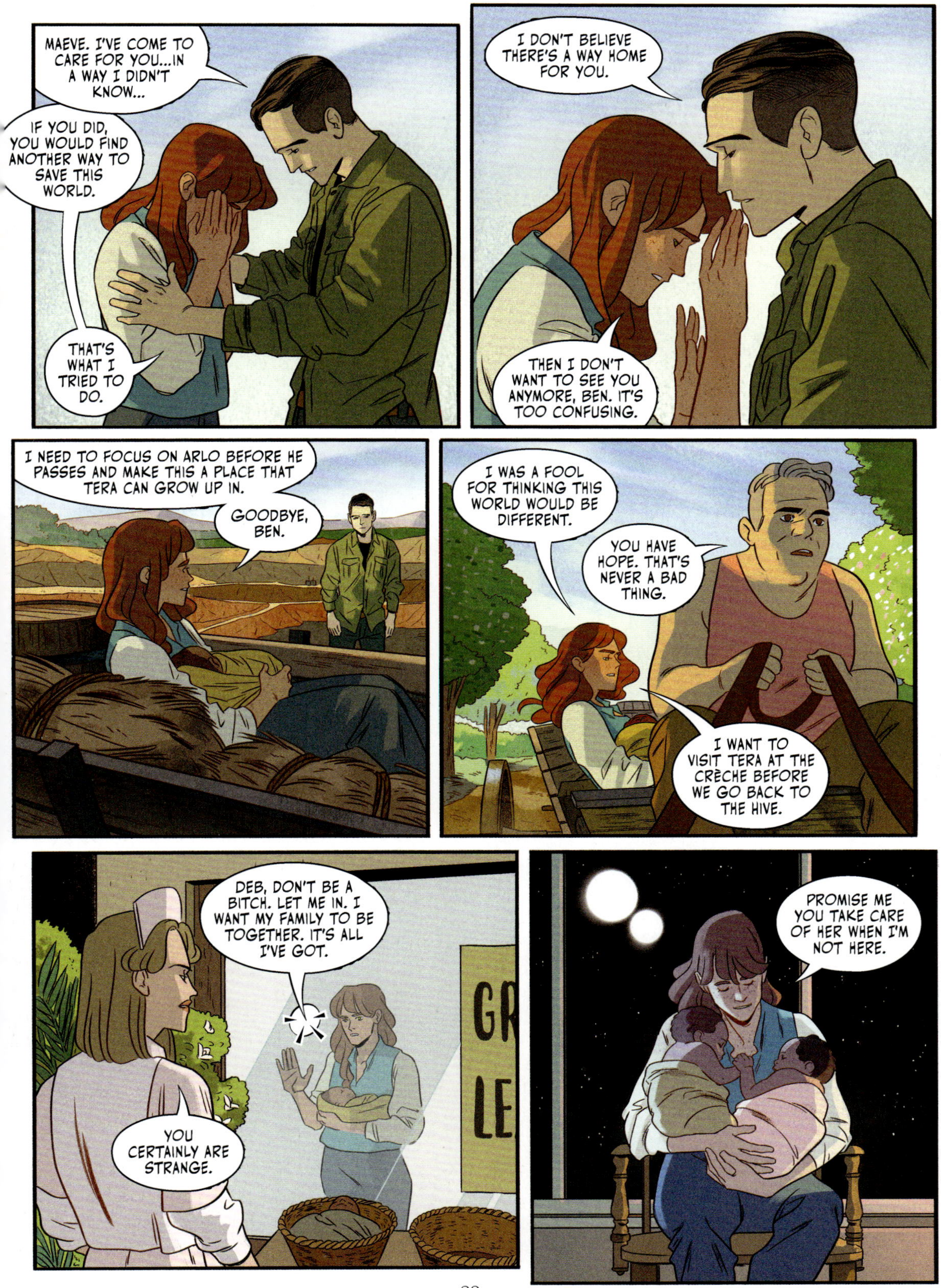
MAEVE. I'VE COME TO CARE FOR YOU...IN A WAY I DIDN'T KNOW...
IF YOU DID, YOU WOULD FIND ANOTHER WAY TO SAVE THIS WORLD.
THAT'S WHAT I TRIED TO DO.
I DON'T BELIEVE THERE'S A WAY HOME FOR YOU.
THEN I DON'T WANT TO SEE YOU ANYMORE, BEN. IT'S TOO CONFUSING.
I NEED TO FOCUS ON ARLO BEFORE HE PASSES AND MAKE THIS A PLACE THAT TERA CAN GROW UP IN.
GOODBYE, BEN.
I WAS A FOOL FOR THINKING THIS WORLD WOULD BE DIFFERENT.
YOU HAVE HOPE. THAT'S NEVER A BAD THING.
I WANT TO VISIT TERA AT THE CRÈCHE BEFORE WE GO BACK TO THE HIVE.
DEB, DON'T BE A BITCH. LET ME IN. I WANT MY FAMILY TO BE TOGETHER. IT'S ALL I'VE GOT.
YOU CERTAINLY ARE STRANGE.
PROMISE ME YOU TAKE CARE OF HER WHEN I'M NOT HERE.

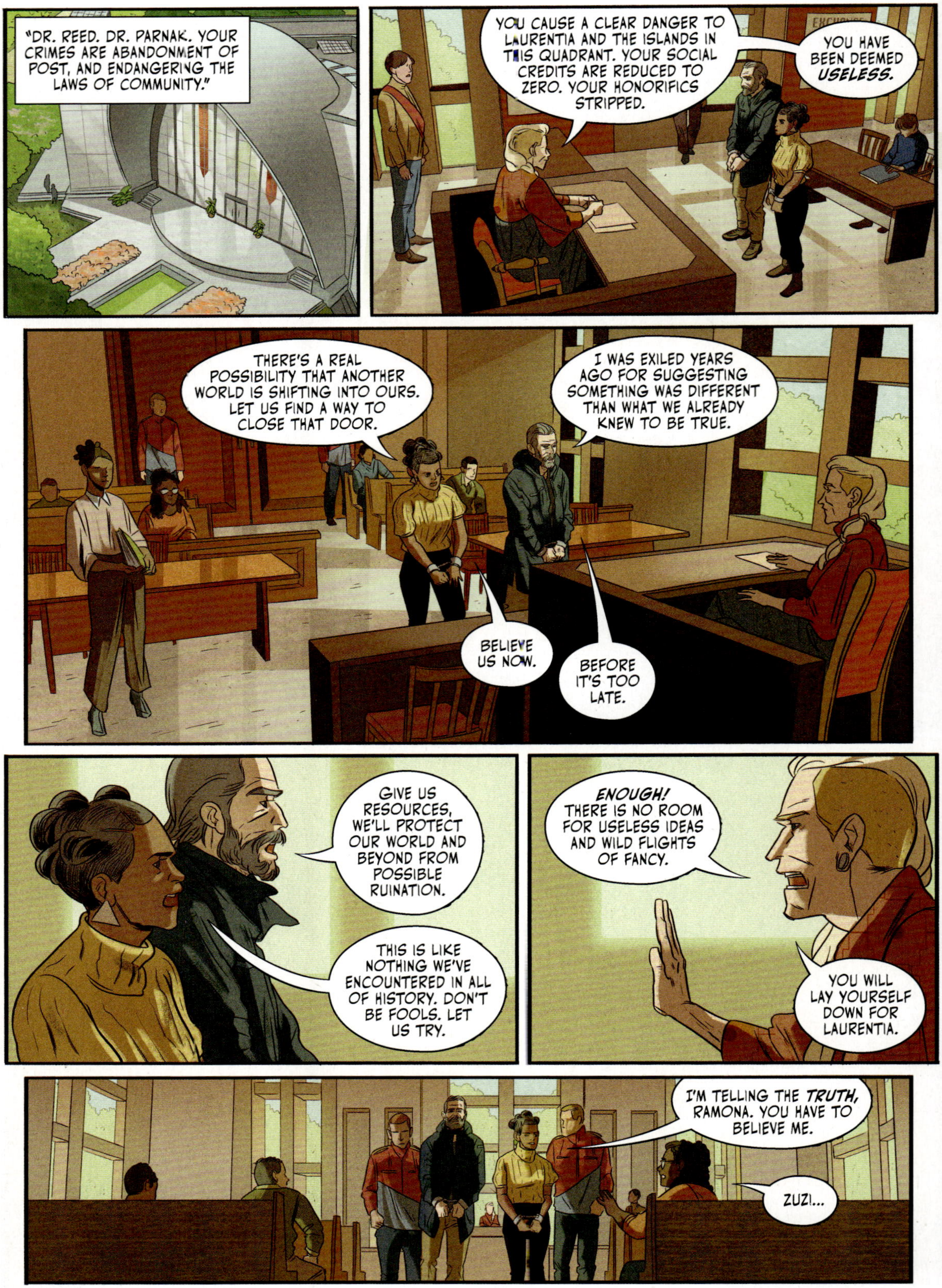
"DR. REED. DR. PARNAK. YOUR CRIMES ARE ABANDONMENT OF POST, AND ENDANGERING THE LAWS OF COMMUNITY."
YOU CAUSE A CLEAR DANGER TO LAURENTIA AND THE ISLANDS IN THIS QUADRANT. YOUR SOCIAL CREDITS ARE REDUCED TO ZERO. YOUR HONORIFICS STRIPPED.
YOU HAVE BEEN DEEMED *USELESS.*
THERE'S A REAL POSSIBILITY THAT ANOTHER WORLD IS SHIFTING INTO OURS. LET US FIND A WAY TO CLOSE THAT DOOR.
I WAS EXILED YEARS AGO FOR SUGGESTING SOMETHING WAS DIFFERENT THAN WHAT WE ALREADY KNEW TO BE TRUE.
BELIEVE US NOW.
BEFORE IT'S TOO LATE.
GIVE US RESOURCES, WE'LL PROTECT OUR WORLD AND BEYOND FROM POSSIBLE RUINATION.
THIS IS LIKE NOTHING WE'VE ENCOUNTERED IN ALL OF HISTORY. DON'T BE FOOLS. LET US TRY.
ENOUGH! THERE IS NO ROOM FOR USELESS IDEAS AND WILD FLIGHTS OF FANCY.
YOU WILL LAY YOURSELF DOWN FOR LAURENTIA.
I'M TELLING THE *TRUTH,* RAMONA. YOU HAVE TO BELIEVE ME.
ZUZI...

DON'T WORRY, RAMONA. I'LL TALK TO MADAME PREMIERE.
...I PULLED HER FROM A PORTAL IN THE WOODS. SHE WAS DISORIENTED. IN DISTRESS.
YOUR BONDMATE?
YES.
THAT IS QUITE A TALL TALE.
I BELIEVE MAEVE LINDHOLM IS A VISITOR FROM ANOTHER WORLD.
WHY DID YOU KEEP THIS FROM ME? INFORMATION IS OF USE.
I SHOULD HAVE TOLD YOU THIS SOONER.
I THOUGHT SHE WAS A SPY LOST IN THE STORM. I TOOK HER POSSESSIONS AND DUMPED HER IN THE RIVER.
BUT SHE WAS BROUGHT TO VERDELINA, SO I CHANGED TACTICS, KEPT HER CLOSE...
SURVEILLING HER THROUGH YOUR EMOTIONAL CONNECTION. I SEE.
WALK ME THROUGH THIS RIDICULOUS PROOF OF YOURS.
MACHINES THAT FLY. MOTORS THAT ACHIEVE HIGH SPEEDS. CITIES THAT LIGHT UP INDEPENDENT OF THE SUN OR THE WIND.
THEY HAVE EVEN TRAVELLED TO THE MOONS.
IF WE COULD GET THAT TECH-NOLOGY TO SURVIVE A CYCLE INTACT, WE COULD INCAPACITATE OTHER ISLANDS...
THEY'D BE DEPENDENT ON US. WE NEED TO EXPLOIT THIS.
THEN I NEED YOUR PERMISSION TO GET THOSE SCIENTISTS.

I SPENT SO MUCH TIME WITH MY THEORIES, I WORRIED I'D BE RECLAIMED ALONE.
I'M GLAD I'M WITH YOU TOO, AL.
WHATEVER HAPPENS WITH THE PORTAL, IT'S OUT OF OUR HANDS NOW.
I'M SORRY WE COULDN'T SEE OUR WORK THROUGH.
I WOULD'VE LIKED TO SEE HOW IT PLAYED OUT.
IF THERE'S A PATTERN...
MAY THE MOONS NOW HELP THE LIVING.
STOP! CEASE THE CEREMONY. OFFICIAL BUSINESS BY THE COMMAND OF MADAME PREMIERE.
I'M LOOKING FOR DR. ZUZI REED.
I'M DR. REED.
I NEED INFORMATION ABOUT YOUR THEORY OF OTHER, PARALLEL WORLDS.
THIS PORTAL--CAN IT BE OPENED FOR ONE TO TRAVEL THROUGH?
THEORETICALLY, BUT THE CONDITIONS AREN'T RIGHT. WAIT. IS SOMEONE TRAPPED HERE ALIVE?
THAT'S THE VARIABLE. IT'S AN IMBALANCE!
THAT'S WHAT KEPT IT OPEN THIS TIME.
DR. REED PLEASE COME WITH ME.
WE'RE A TEAM. I WON'T GO WITHOUT HIM.
I'M SORRY. I ONLY HAVE A REPRIEVE IN HAND FOR YOU.
GO. YOU HAVE MORE LIVING TO DO, ZUZI. MAKE ME PROUD.

WE'LL DEBRIEF WITH MADAME PREMIERE. YOU'LL FILL HER IN ON THE POWER WE CAN GET FROM THE OTHER SIDE.
FUNNY. I SPENT YEARS TRYING TO GET HER TO TAKE ME SERIOUSLY.
WE'LL GET YOU A LAB TO FIGURE OUT WAYS TO HARNESS AND EXPLOIT THAT POWER.
WHEN THERE'S DOWNTIME, YOU'LL HELP MY FRIEND AND HER BABIES GET HOME.
BABIES. THAT'S THE VARIABLE. THEY'RE OF BOTH WORLDS.
BUT NO, YOUR TIMELINE WON'T WORK.
WHY NOT? THERE MUST BE A WAY TO ACTIVATE THAT KINETIC ENERGY.
THE WORLDS ARE ON TOP OF EACH OTHER, LIKE THE PAGES OF A BOOK. THE LETTERS LINE UP BUT ARE A LITTLE OFF.
SHIT. DR. PARNAK COULD EXPLAIN IT BETTER.
THE STARS I SAW IN THE RIPPED SKY WERE FROM A *YEAR* IN THE FUTURE.
WHICH IS IN THE NEXT FEW DAYS. SHE'D HAVE TO GO THEN.
DO YOU THINK YOU CAN MAKE IT HAPPEN. GET HER HOME?
MADAME PREMIERE WILL HAVE MY HEAD FOR THIS.
IF SO, THERE'S NO TIME TO WASTE.

I'VE COME TO LOVE IT HERE. THE CLEAR SKIES, THE ABUNDANT GREENERY, THE SOUNDS. IT'S IDYLLIC. EVEN THOUGH I'VE LEARNED SOME HARD TRUTHS ABOUT YOUR SOCIETY.
CAN YOU TELL ME ABOUT YOUR WORLD? ABOUT THOSE THINGS THAT I SAW.
WHAT WE'VE ACHIEVED IS INCREDIBLE. FLIGHT. SPACE EXPLORATION. COMPUTERS. QUANTUM PHYSICS.
THOSE WORDS SOUND LIKE MY DREAMS. TRAVELING IN SPACE...
BUT WE BOTCHED IT ALL UP. SPECIES SUICIDE.
BUT SURELY YOUR SCIENTISTS AND THINKERS COULD TEACH PEOPLE?
NOT EVERYONE LISTENS.
STILL. I'D DO ANYTHING TO SAVE MY CHILDREN. EVEN IF IT MEANS GOING BACK THERE.
NOTHING IS CERTAIN, BUT IF THERE'S A CHANCE FOR THAT AND TO SHUT THE PORTAL, IT'S SOON.
I'LL GET READY THEN.
YOUR WORLD, MAEVE. IT SOUNDS WONDERFUL AND TERRIBLE.
I DREAD GOING BACK THERE.
BUT IT'S ARLO'S ONLY CHANCE.

THEN WE'LL DO OUR BEST TO GET YOU THERE.
I'M SAD YOU'LL LEAVE US JUST AS I'M KNOWING YOU. JEALOUS EVEN.
WHY? IT'S LIKE THE APOCALYPSE THERE.
EVERYWHERE CAN SEEM LIKE A NIGHTMARE DEPENDING ON WHERE YOU'RE COMING FROM.
THE DIFFERENCE IS HOW YOU DREAM ABOUT THE FUTURE. HOW YOU FIND HOPE IN THE DISMAL.
YOU'RE RIGHT.
THANK YOU FOR GIVING MY FAMILY A CHANCE AT A LIFE TOGETHER.
THERE'S ALMOST NOTHING FOR ME HERE. I'M LAUGHED AT AND DISMISSED.
WILL YOU AND BEN SUFFER FOR TRYING TO HELP ME? FOR NOT PROVIDING MADAME PREMIERE THE TECHNOLOGY SHE WANTS TO STEAL?
I'M ALREADY LIVING ON BORROWED TIME. BUT HE'S PUT EVERYTHING ON THE LINE FOR YOU. HE'LL PAY DEARLY.
YOU KNOW, DESPITE ALL YOU'VE TOLD ME I'D LIKE TO SEE YOUR WORLD. SEE YOUR MOON.
WILL YOU TAKE ME WITH YOU?

Dear Ramona, I only have a moment to scratch these words to you. It breaks me that I won't get to say goodbye.
You are the one thing here that lights up my life.
I hope you understand my choice and can forgive me.
I have a chance to go somewhere I can really be of use.
WHAT DO YOU *MEAN* CAPTAIN NAGATA'S MISSING? FIND HIM!
Captain Nagata took a great risk saving me. Please help him.
I know he promised he'd reunite us. But we both know that's impossible even if I stayed.
I am far better for having loved you.

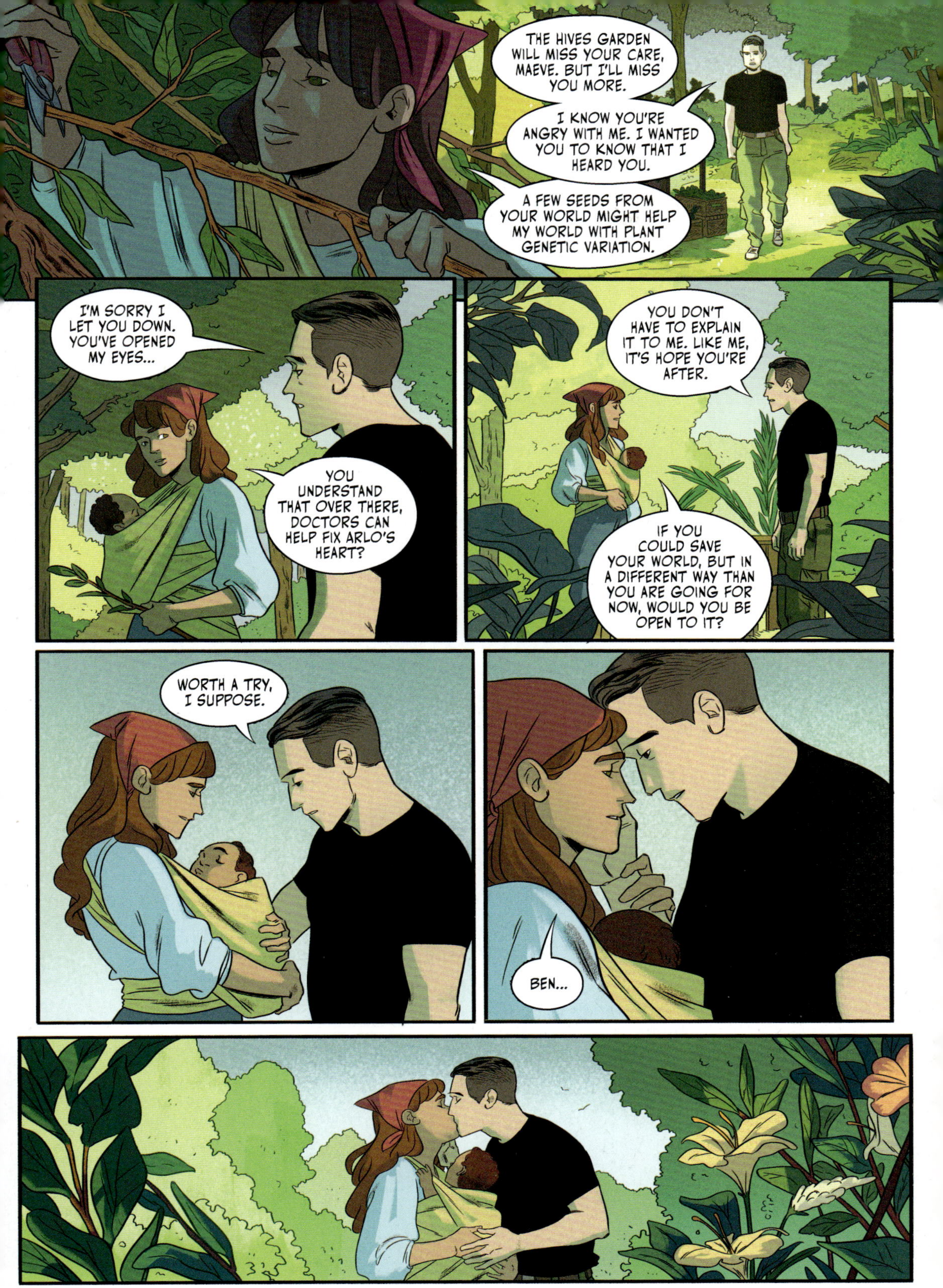
THE HIVES GARDEN WILL MISS YOUR CARE, MAEVE. BUT I'LL MISS YOU MORE.
I KNOW YOU'RE ANGRY WITH ME. I WANTED YOU TO KNOW THAT I HEARD YOU.
A FEW SEEDS FROM YOUR WORLD MIGHT HELP MY WORLD WITH PLANT GENETIC VARIATION.
I'M SORRY I LET YOU DOWN. YOU'VE OPENED MY EYES...
YOU UNDERSTAND THAT OVER THERE, DOCTORS CAN HELP FIX ARLO'S HEART?
YOU DON'T HAVE TO EXPLAIN IT TO ME. LIKE ME, IT'S HOPE YOU'RE AFTER.
IF YOU COULD SAVE YOUR WORLD, BUT IN A DIFFERENT WAY THAN YOU ARE GOING FOR NOW, WOULD YOU BE OPEN TO IT?
WORTH A TRY, I SUPPOSE.
BEN...

IT'S LIKE AL SAID. THE NIGHT BECOMES AS BRIGHT AS DAY.
THIS IS IT.
WAAH WAAH
MAEVE!
IT'S TIME, ISN'T IT?
I THOUGHT WE HAD A COUPLE OF DAYS.
THIS IS NOT AN EXACT SCIENCE.
I'M NOT READY. I STILL HAVE TO GET TERA. PREPARE MORE PLANT TISSUE SAMPLES...
I'M SORRY, MAEVE. IT'S NOW OR NEVER.
IT'S YOUR CHOICE, OF COURSE. YOU EITHER STAY HERE OR WE TRY TO GO.
WE GO.

YOU CAME THROUGH THAT? IT LOOKS LIKE IT'S TEARING EVERYTHING APART!
IT GOT ME THROUGH HERE IN ONE PIECE, IT'LL GET ME AND ARLO BACK.
IT'S STILL CHAOS. IT DOESN'T LOOK SAFE.
IT IS. FOR THE MOMENT. I JUST *KNOW* IT.
BUT WE MUST GO NOW!

IT'S REAL. IT'S A WHOLE OTHER WORLD. I CAN SEE SOMETHING...
KEEP ARLO SAFE WHILE I SAY MY GOODBYES.
MAKE IT QUICK. ITS PROPERTIES ARE ALREADY CHANGING.
THANK YOU FOR WELCOMING ME HERE. TELL TERA ABOUT ME WHEN SHE GROWS UP.
TELL HER I'M SORRY.
WE'LL LOOK AFTER HER AS WE DID YOU.
GO! DON'T MISS YOUR CHANCE.
MAEVE! HURRY!

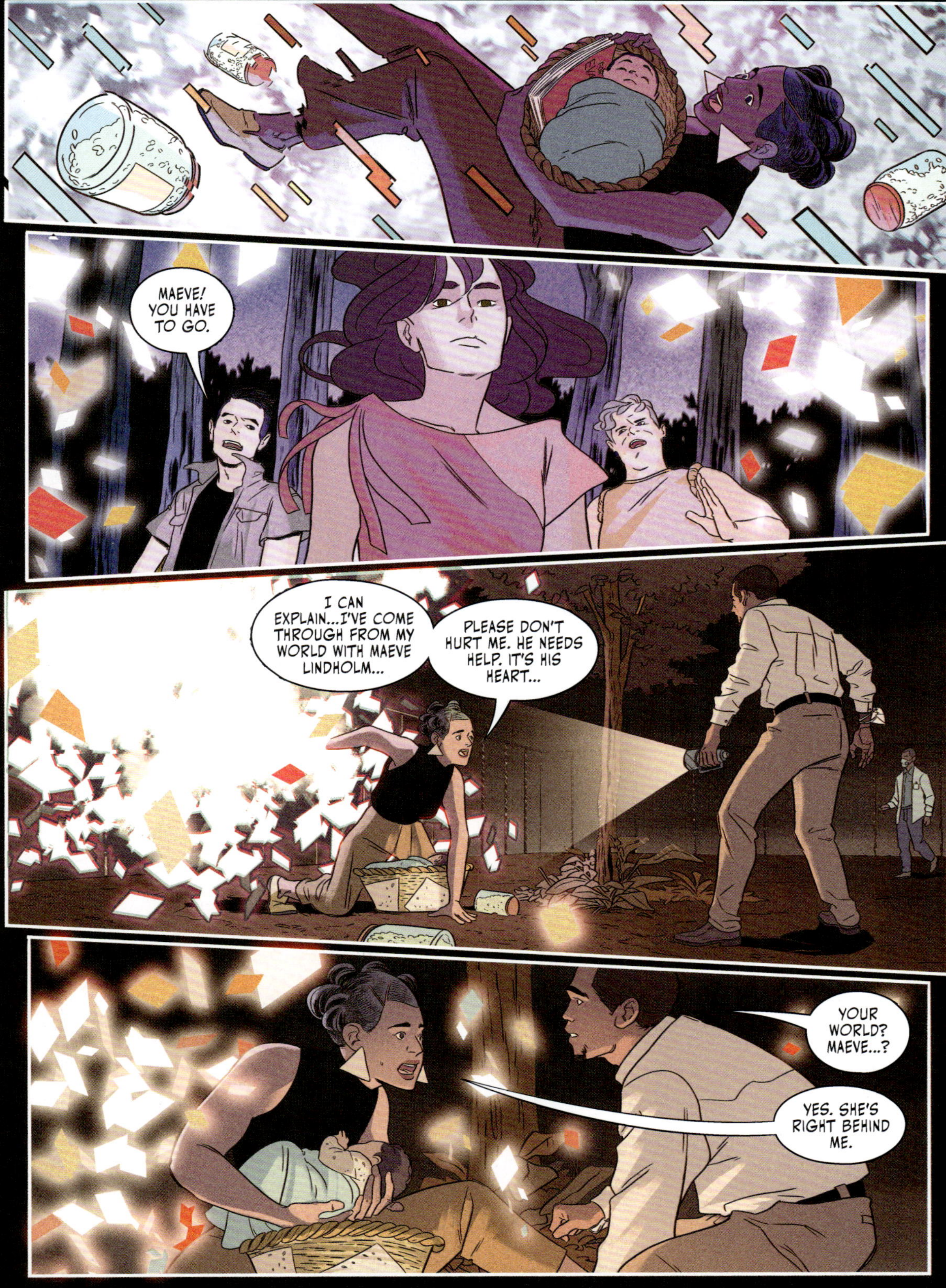
MAEVE! YOU HAVE TO GO.
I CAN EXPLAIN...I'VE COME THROUGH FROM MY WORLD WITH MAEVE LINDHOLM...
PLEASE DON'T HURT ME. HE NEEDS HELP. IT'S HIS HEART...
YOUR WORLD? MAEVE...?
YES. SHE'S RIGHT BEHIND ME.

MAEVE! SHE'S THERE! MAEVE!
GRAB MY HAND!
MAEVE!
I TOLD HER TO HURRY, OR SHE'D MISS THE WINDOW.
I HAVE HER THINGS. HER SEEDS. THEY'RE FROM MY WORLD. SHE SAID THEY WOULD HELP.
SEEDS...
YOU MUST BE EVAN...THIS IS HER CHILD.
CHILD? SHE'S ONLY BEEN GONE A FEW HOURS...
MAEVE'S BEEN ON OUR WORLD FOR OVER A YEAR.
FOR EVAN
GOODBYE.

AND THAT'S HOW YOU CAME TO ME, ARLO. FROM YOUR MOTHER LOST ON ANOTHER WORLD. AND SHE GAVE US THE TOOLS TO TRY MAKE A CHANGE...
THE END IS THE START OF HOPE.
AND I THOUGHT OF YOU TERA WHEN I DIDN'T LEAVE. I THOUGHT I CAN'T SAVE US FROM OURSELVES, BUT I CAN HELP HERE AND *THERE* UNTIL PEOPLE BELIEVE.
AND WE CAN TRY TO REMAKE THIS WORLD.
WE ARE THE SEEDS.
DR. REED TO MOONBASE ONE. WHAT A VIEW.

"MAMA."
"PAPA."
"TELL ME THE STORY AGAIN..."
"IT FELT LIKE IT WAS THE BEGINNING OF THE END."
"AN END IS A BEGINNING, THOUGH."
"YES, THAT'S RIGHT. IT IS."

Flavia Biondi
Cover Sketches

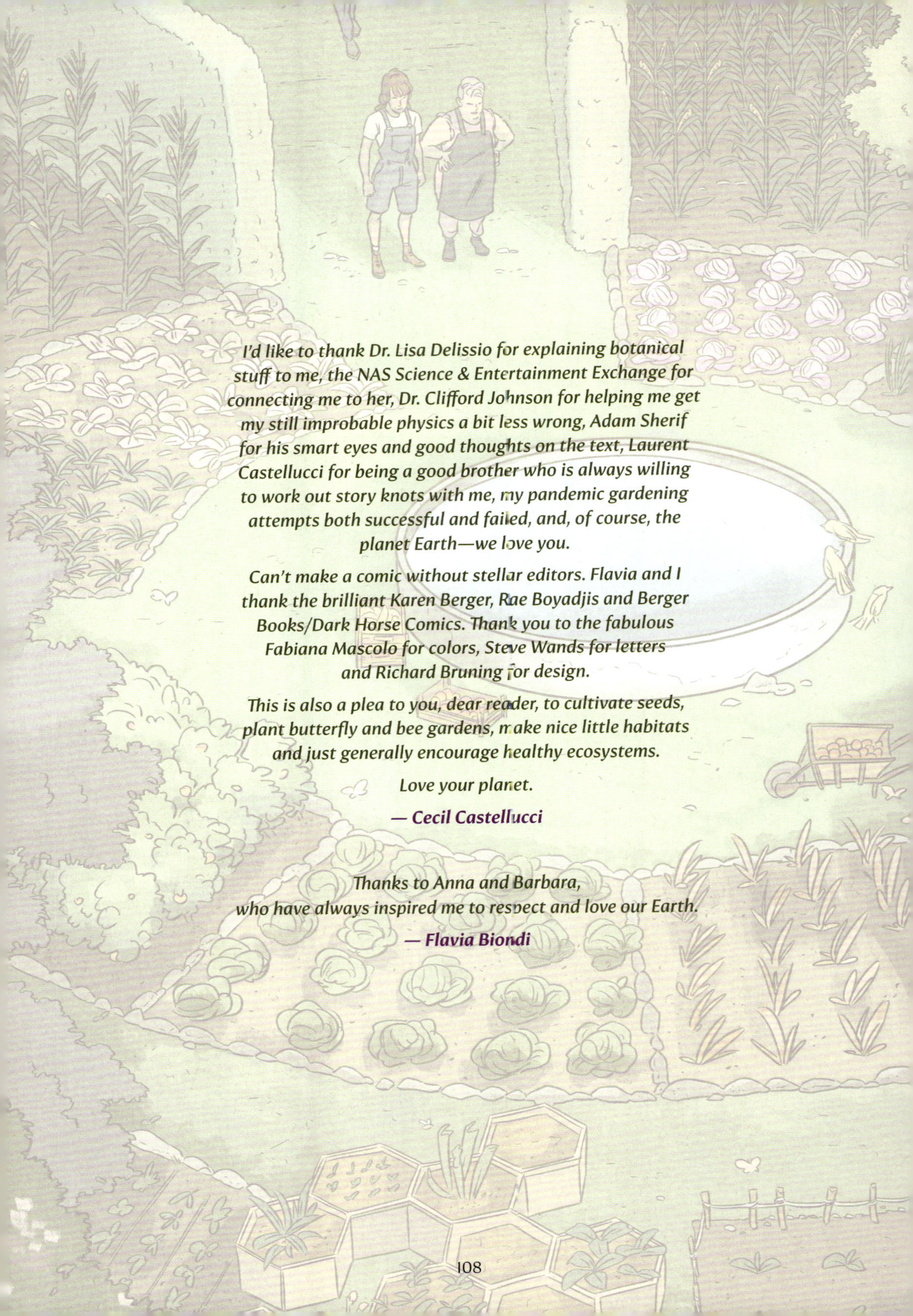

I'd like to thank Dr. Lisa Delissio for explaining botanical stuff to me, the NAS Science & Entertainment Exchange for connecting me to her, Dr. Clifford Johnson for helping me get my still improbable physics a bit less wrong, Adam Sherif for his smart eyes and good thoughts on the text, Laurent Castellucci for being a good brother who is always willing to work out story knots with me, my pandemic gardening attempts both successful and failed, and, of course, the planet Earth—we love you.

Can't make a comic without stellar editors. Flavia and I thank the brilliant Karen Berger, Rae Boyadjis and Berger Books/Dark Horse Comics. Thank you to the fabulous Fabiana Mascolo for colors, Steve Wands for letters and Richard Bruning for design.

This is also a plea to you, dear reader, to cultivate seeds, plant butterfly and bee gardens, make nice little habitats and just generally encourage healthy ecosystems.

Love your planet.

— Cecil Castellucci

Thanks to Anna and Barbara,
who have always inspired me to respect and love our Earth.

— Flavia Biondi

Cecil Castellucci

ERIC CHARLES

is an award-winning and *New York Times* best-selling author of books and graphic novels for young adults including ***Shade, The Changing Girl, The Plain Janes*** and ***Soupy Leaves Home***. Her short stories and comics have been published in Strange Horizons, Tor.com, and many other anthologies. She has also written three opera librettos. She is a two-time MacDowell Fellow. She splits her time between Los Angeles and Montreal.

Flavia Biondi

is a comic artist, illustrator and teacher based in Bologna, Italy. Since 2012 she has collaborated with the artistic label Manticora Autoproduzioni and various publishers such as Renbooks, BAO Publishing, Renape, Sergio Bonelli Editore and Berger Books. ***Shifting Earth*** is her second graphic novel with Berger Books, after ***Ruby Falls***.

Fabiana Mascolo

is a visual artist based in Rome. She's been working in the comics industry since 2015, collaborating with publishers such as BOOM! Studios, Dark Horse, Èdtions Soleil, Sergio Bonelli Editore and more. Her recent publications include ***Magic: The Hidden Planeswalker***, ***Firefly Brand New Verse*** and ***Yasmeen***.

Steve Wands

is a Harvey Award-nominated and Lammy Award-winning comic book letterer for DC Comics, Image, TKO Studios, Dark Horse, and others. He's also the author of the ***Stay Dead*** series, ***Night Of The Drunks***, and co-writer of ***Trail of Blood***. His work appears in titles like the mega-hit manga ***Attack on Titan***, ***Batman***, ***The Flash***, ***Gideon Falls***, and many others. For Berger Books, he has also lettered ***Ruby Falls*** and ***Everything***.

BERGER BOOKS™

ANTHONY BOURDAIN'S HUNGRY GHOSTS
One night, chefs gather to outscare each other with tantalizing tales of fear and food—but will they surviv

POST YORK
In a New York City drowned in its past, Crosby fights not just to survive... but to fully live. When he meets mysterious Ivy, the way he lives will change forever—but will it be for the better?

SHE COULD FLY Vol. One
A fantastic, unknown flying woman suddenly explodes mid-air—and crashes into the life of disturbed teen Luna Brewster.

SHE COULD FLY Vol. Two
Luna follows the flying woman's broken trail to find the truth—and to save herself. But is she too far gone?

SHE COULD FLY Vol. Three
In the shocking conclusion of the series, a new, dangerous Flying Woman has come to terrorize Chicago—and it's Luna's turn to take control.

RUBY FALLS
Unlikely detective Lana Blake uncovers three generations of deadly small-town secrets.

EVERYTHING Vol. One
A mysterious superstore arrives in a small town... and catalyzes a horrifying pursuit of happiness.

EVERYTHING Vol. Two
As the Everything store gains power, so do its renegade opponents—but only one side can win this battle for The American Dream.

THE SEEDS

When an alien falls in love with a human, a journalist stumbles into the story of a lifetime, but reporting it just might destroy planet Earth.

EISNER & HUGO AWARD WINNER

LAGUARDIA

In an alien-integrated world, pregnant doctor Future Nwafor Chukwuebuka smuggles an illegal, sentient plant through LaGuardia International and Interstellar Airport, which changes her life forever.

A Deluxe Hardcover edition packed with extras including a script chapter, behind-the-scenes art section, and more!

Also available in trade paperback.

EISNER AWARD WINNER

INVISIBLE KINGDOM Vol. One

A young religious acolyte and a dogged freighter pilot uncover an inconceivable conspiracy between a world's major religion and the mega corporation that controls society.

INVISIBLE KINGDOM Vol. Two

With only part of the truth blown open and bigger secrets looming, will Vess and Grix become stronger —or shatter apart?

INVISIBLE KINGDOM Vol. Three

The breathtaking tale of the *Sundog* concludes, and Vess and Grix are faced with a new choice: love... or destruction.

REWILD

A self-proclaimed fairy changeling gives the world a choice: appease a race of rageful fae . . . or else.

INCOGNEGRO: A GRAPHIC MYSTERY

Zane Pinchback goes "incognegro" to investigate his brother's arrest in a fast-paced exploration of race and identity.

INCOGNEGRO: RENAISSANCE

Our race-bending protagonist penetrates a world where he feels stranger than ever before.

EDITOR
Karen Berger

ASSOCIATE EDITOR
Rae Boyadjis

BOOK DESIGNER
Richard Bruning

DIGITAL ART TECHNICIAN
Adam Pruett

PRESIDENT & PUBLISHER
Mike Richardson

Published by Dark Horse Comics LLC
10956 SE Main Street, Milwaukie, Oregon 97222

First Edition: June 2022
ISBN: 978-1-50672-910-7
Digital ISBN: 978-1-50672-911-4
Printed in China

DarkHorse.com
Comicshoplocator.com

Library of Congress Cataloging-in-Publication Data
Names: Castellucci, Cecil, 1969- author. | Biondi, Flavia, 1988- artist. |Mascolo, Fabiana, colorist.
Title: Shifting Earth / script, Cecil Castellucci ; art, Flavia Biondi ; colors, Fabiana Mascolo.
Description: First edition. | Milwaukie, Oregon : Berger Books/Dark Horse Books, 2022. |
Identifiers: LCCN 2021059694 | ISBN 9781506729107 (trade paperback) | ISBN 9781506729114 (ebook)
Subjects: LCGFT: Science fiction comics. | Graphic novels.
Classification: LCC PN6727.C389 S45 2022 | DDC 741.5/973--dc23/eng/20220204
LC record available at https://lccn.loc.gov/2021059694